Paulina & Fran

A NOVEL

Rachel B. Glaser

GRANTA

Granta Publications, 12 Addison Avenue, London W11 4QR

First published in Great Britain by Granta Books, 2015
First published in the United States by Harper Perennial,
HarperCollins, 2015

A CIP catalogue record for this book is available from the British Library.

1 3 5 7 9 10 8 6 4 2

ISBN 978 1 78378 158 4 (trade paperback)
ISBN 978 1 78378 160 7 (ebook)

Designed by Sunil Manchikanti

Offset by Avon DataSet, Bidford on Avon, Warwickshire B50 4JH

Printed and bound by CPI Group (UK) Ltd, Croydon, CR0 4YY

www.grantabooks.com

FOR CAITLIN & KATHLEEN

All the girls knew how to dance. There were barely any boys and the boys were soft or vain or so sought after that they seemed cliché or used. This was all in a cold, cold town. People moved to the college and their families forgot about them. Snowflakes died on their faces. They endured the human struggle.

Paulina & Fran

1

Paulina was dissatisfied with her lover. He was too tall. He leaned on things. He thought he knew everything. Lying next to his sleeping body, Paulina considered his narrow, serious nose. The sheet was pulled to his waist, exposing a pale chest—like a CPR mannequin, she thought. She moved to feel if Julian was hard, but his penis was mushy in her hand. She dropped it and rose to her feet.

Paulina fluffed her curly, shoulder-length hair. She knew that curly hair was the hair of creative geniuses. It was a mark of originality in a woman, though she found it frivolous on a man. She yanked off her nightgown and stuffed herself into a tight dress from SUPERTHRIFT. It was long and virginal in a daydreamy, Renaissance-fair way, but with satisfaction she cut it to show her thighs. The remnants of the dress—strips of netting and cheap satin—she threw in the garbage over the ruins of last night's dinner.

Julian mumbled in his sleep. Paulina nudged him and he

didn't wake. Julian slept through everything, even her industrial hair dryer. Months ago, she'd picked him up in the college library, initially impressed by his height, surprised when he had brains, a voice, a way of slouching that showed disappointment in the world. Paulina took a pen from her nightstand, then scrawled her name on his bicep and drew a wreath of flowers around it. His water glass was empty and she found herself walking to the sink to fill it, though this was something she refused to do when asked.

Paulina studied herself in the mirror, admiring her hair, which hung in elegant auburn curls, but faulting the dress for failing to express her mood. She felt a big ambition, a great horniness, the conviction that she was a genius, and pride in not knowing what kind. She wasn't beautiful, she knew, but she was striking. Her face was not easily forgotten.

Paulina listened to the washing machine's low rumbling from the basement. She threw off the dress and pulled the nightgown back on. She drew firmly on her eyelids with her eye pencil, then put on a massive fur coat. It weighed on her like the next decade. "Good-bye, Brains," she said, then left.

Paulina walked quickly, anticipating the boys at Angel's party—each the keeper of his own tepid garden. She smelled them in her classes. She slept with the boys in bathrooms at parties, in parked cars in the SUPERTHRIFT parking lot, in the woods behind the college library. She kept seeing Julian out of habit, but slowly he was becoming a souvenir to her, something better off sealed in resin and hidden in the back of her drawer. She imagined saying this to Sadie and Allison, both of whom she hadn't seen for almost a week.

Across the street, an intimidating girl Paulina called the Venus Flytrap was covered with face paint and bearing the cold with hard nipples. Paulina shrank back in her fur coat. Oblivious to Paulina, the Venus Flytrap walked gaily in the other direction. One drunken night after Paulina jauntily linked arms with her, the girl had said coldly, "Just because we have friends in common doesn't mean we must be friends." It had been a stunning rejection, one Paulina wanted to try on someone else.

Paulina expected cheers when she walked in. "I have arrived," she said loudly. "Straight from my bed." She was instantly disappointed. Acquaintances were scattered around the small apartment. Grating techno blared from another room. Paulina looked expectantly for Sadie and Allison and waited to be found.

Paintings filled up a whole wall salon style. Paulina studied them—messy landscapes and muddy, vague portraits—automatically critiquing them in her head. Which best created the illusion of light? Questions like this had been eerily placed inside her by a charcoal-covered man who awed them and taught drawing. The school was one entirely focused on visual art. The students had a skimpy understanding of the world. If they'd followed current events before, if they'd known math, this information dimmed and dissolved. Here, any danceable music was exalted. A tidal wave of nostalgia knocked everyone over before anything even happened.

Paulina flung her arms around Sadie, an excitable apparel major. Sadie was obvious. She beamed when she said something worthwhile. She had butt-length black hair and bangs. Whereas Paulina was curvy, or one could say sturdy, or even, as her enemies would say, chubby, Sadie was thin with small breasts that bounced braless in her shirt. "Is that a nightgown?" Sadie asked.

"Julian prefers a child's bedtime," Paulina said.

"I thought you were breaking up with him."

"Every house needs a house cat," Paulina replied. Sadie laughed. Paulina felt glad they were friends. Sadie launched into a story about a boy she had met on vacation. As Paulina listened she looked Sadie up and down, wincing when she saw the red leather boots. Years ago, Paulina had stolen them off a scarecrow, but had sacrificed them to Sadie in exchange for completing her design homework freshman year. The boots pinched the feet of whoever wore them, but gave the wearer power. For the hundredth time, Paulina regretted the trade. A dull pull tugged at her mood.

"Where's Tim?" asked Paulina. Tim was a tall, confident furniture major. Sadie shrugged. "The things I would do to Tim," Paulina sung in a low voice.

"He's with Cassie!" Sadie said.

"Who?" Paulina asked with mock curiosity.

Allison walked over and gave Paulina a beer. Allison was a painting major with bleak, depressing hair. She was imposingly withdrawn. Though Paulina had looked forward to seeing her, her capacity for enthusiasm was diminished by Sadie's boots. Paulina gave Allison an empty hug, then stiffened when she spotted a boy with glasses whom she'd seduced and regretted in the girls' cafeteria bathroom. "That beast follows me," she muttered.

"Which one?" asked Sadie, turning.

Paulina dismissed her with a wave of her hand. The party showed no potential. The music was alienating. Paulina retreated into the palace of herself. She needed to end it with Julian. He was weighing her down. He was ruining her. She looked frantically for Tim, nearly making eye contact with the beast.

"I'm bored," she announced, sweating in her coat.

"Maybe this will get fun," Sadie said and did a dinky dance in her boots.

"Is there anything happening at the Color Club?" Allison asked.

"I'd know if there was," Paulina said, finishing her beer. She watched two girls from her art history class try to convince a boy to dance. She overheard a girl named Eileen say, "He wrote his dad an e-mail to tell him not to kiss him on the neck."

Allison walked over another beer for Paulina. The three girls were silent. People they knew talked and laughed around them, but they stood like trees. Someone complained about a bad crit he'd had, and someone else one-upped him with a worse crit she'd had. Sadie played solemnly with the fringe on her skirt, and then the fringe on her shirt.

Paulina watched Sadie and Allison dance around a hairless boy who made tribal masks. Initially, Allison and Sadie were solely friends with Paulina and merely tolerated each other, but when Paulina started dating Julian, Sadie and Allison became genuinely close. They enjoyed simple things Paulina abhorred—walking for the sake of walking, working side by side, and long, leisurely lunches at Thai Dream.

"Aren't they uncomfortable?" Paulina asked.

"What?" Sadie said, dancing.

"The boots."

"I love them," Sadie said.

Paulina was in disbelief that anyone could dance at such a lackluster party. I should be running through a field, she thought. I should be drafting my will. I could be betting on horses. She imagined there was a car outside waiting for her. "Just drive," she'd tell the driver in a sultry voice. "Drive until we run out of gas," and the driver would be Tim.

A powerful boredom pushed Paulina into Angel's kitchen. Though she wasn't hungry, she searched the cabinets for something to eat. She was thirsty and she was dizzy. On the counter was a vial of orchid food she thought she could use in her latest homemade conditioner. She put it in her coat pocket and drifted into the bathroom. Shoving aside the shampoos and lotions, she found a mud cream from the Dead Sea and read its label.

She crouched in the bathtub, feeling faint, noting the faded ring of dirt. Paulina closed her eyes and remembered buying her coat at a vintage shop she had believed at the time to be mystical, when she believed in such things. But what was she thinking? She still believed things to be mystical. She always guessed the correct time on a clock. Certain foods gave her visions. Paulina weakly pulled the shower curtain shut. Sweat dotted her hairline. A sun burned behind her eyes.

"Party at the Color Club!"

They ran down the street in a pack. Sadie's face was lost in a dream. "What's with her?" Paulina asked.

"She met a boy," Allison said, "on the train—"

"Oh yes, the train," Paulina said, striding ahead.

"We forgot Gretchen!" a boy said and stopped, but no one went back.

They passed old Victorian houses. Paulina hugged her fur. The cold air stung their faces. Occasionally a car drove past, its headlights thrilling Paulina.

"What's Color Club?" a small graphic design major asked, and Paulina pitied her.

"Club Homo?" Sadie said. "Have you heard of that?"

The girl shook her head.

"Do you know that beautiful boy Dean? Angelic face, really funny?" Sadie asked.

"Sort of," the girl said.

They passed people they knew and the group got bigger. "What about Troy? He looks like a nutcracker figurine."

Paulina shut out the clueless graphic designer. The boys at the Color Club were the coolest guys in school. They weren't hippies or punks, or part of any group. They were unlike the mainstream gays one got used to. They'd formed a woozy cult-like community. There were drugs, but that was only some of it. There were rocks in their bathtub, cats with dyed hair. Their clique was like a dance song—catchy, violent, beating with life.

Paulina, Sadie, and Allison had spent their sophomore year discovering this house and the boys inside. Sadie squealed each time the boys drove by in their old van, blasting "the song"—their theme for a while—a seductive redemption song sung by an electric, androgynous voice, recorded in the eighties then forgotten. Paulina scolded Sadie and Allison for being obsessed with them, but Dean&Troy was the password to her college e-mail account.

"They're like sexy orphans," Paulina said.

The graphic designer made a face. "Dean is gay?" she asked.

"Everyone is gay," said Eileen. Paulina had yet to form an opinion of her.

Far from the college, they walked past Portuguese bakeries and soccer fields of dead grass. Before she could see the house, Paulina felt the beat through her shoes. The house was big and crumbling in places. Dream catchers and colored glass hung haphazardly from the porch beams. A painting had been smashed into a tree and remained there, gathering rain and leaves, breeding mold.

Inside, the house was hot from bodies. The living room was dark and empty of furniture. Paulina immediately separated herself from the group she'd come with. There was beer and she took one. Everyone looked good at the Color Club—everyone danced. No one hunched in the corner making small talk. A boy Paulina had once made out with was wearing a

George Washington wig and making out with the Venus Fly-trap. Paulina could hear Sadie speaking loudly over the music, again about the boy she'd met on the train, and how they'd kissed in their seats.

Paulina ran to Dean, who was dancing in a crowd, his face coated with paint. "Paulina!" he shouted. "Sadie!" he screamed. Dean was as nimble and high-spirited as a teen-age girl, and revered like a gay Christ. Paulina hugged Dean and Troy and felt drunk. Paulina searched the room for Zane, a boy so filled with good feeling that, using the bow on her dress, Paulina had once tied herself to him on the dance floor.

The Color Club boys were exactly who Paulina wanted to surround herself with. Her whole life had been a search for charisma like theirs. Unable to seduce them, she'd tried to be their best friend, but the Venus Flytrap had gotten there first. She lived with the boys and rejected Paulina, once forcibly pushing her out of the house. Paulina made friends with the boys, but she was still unsatisfied. She wanted them to replace Sadie and Allison. She wanted friends she didn't talk shit about to other friends. If such friends existed, they must be boys like these, who seemed famous.

When cars drove by, Paulina saw the faces of her class-mates in brief flashes of light. How necessary everyone seemed at a good party! People who'd looked lifeless at Angel's looked vibrant here, and Paulina wanted to have sex with them all.

Apollo walked by and Sadie trembled with laughter. The figure models at their school were usually unattractive or awkward. They didn't seem clean. Their wrinkles showed up in dark lines on the page. Some sulked in their poses, but not Apollo. He posed with a big walking stick and stared defiantly into the eyes of the figure drawers, who looked away. There was a sharpness to his movements, a fanaticism to his beliefs. Naked at the break, he walked easel to easel looking at the drawings. He was often spotted outside class, shirtless on a patch of campus grass listening to his Walkman, doing his own speed tai chi. He was a celebrity of the school, the subject of countless jokes, while drawings of his body smudged between pages of newsprint, and hung framed in the homes of the students' parents.

"Don't make eye contact!" Sadie whispered to Paulina.

"One day, I'll go where no figure drawer has gone before," Paulina said, watching Apollo, feeling his energy in waves.

Dean and Troy danced violently until they crashed into a mirror. Paulina watched the shards fall in blinking pieces. Dean laughed hysterically.

A girl danced in front of the mirror looking at her broken reflection.

"Farm Girl Fashion Disaster!" Sadie shouted to Paulina.

Paulina slowed to watch the girl's crazed dancing.

"Why 'farm girl'?" Allison asked.

"She caught a frog in the quad once, remember?" Paulina said without turning.

"Her name is Fran," Allison said. "She's in my painting studio."

Paulina had never given this girl much thought when she saw her sashaying across the cafeteria or sleeping through artist talks, but now she saw that the girl's face was beautiful. Her nose wasn't simple. Paulina contemplated the bones of it. Fran's green eyes looked lost. Light, curly hair whipped against her forehead. There was something innovative in the layout of her face, but her expression showed no understanding of this.

Fran was absorbed in her jagged reflection. She wore a short dress with tiny hearts on it, and a man's flannel. Paulina stared, realizing Fran was friends with one of Paulina's enemies. Paulina couldn't remember which girl. Her idea of Fran darkened. She wanted to be her, or be with her, or destroy her. She watched Fran's breasts bounce in her dress. No one in the room seemed connected to her. Her cheeks concealed things.

Paulina felt dizzy and stopped dancing. She felt her own curls, now puffy and disorganized. *She's cool*, a voice said in Paulina's head. "If brain-dead, naïve Valley girls are cool," Paulina said out loud, stalled in place.

"Hey, I'm from the Valley!" Sadie whined.

Paulina mentally pushed beyond Sadie and Allison. *Away*

with the fools that flock my sides, she thought, in a semiconscious daze. Fran danced in a corner seducing the wall. *Fran*, said a voice inside Paulina. For a brief, exhilarating moment, Paulina forgot the name of the boy snoring in her bed. The Venus Flytrap joined Fran and they danced like their hair was on fire.

"What a glutton for attention," Paulina said, turning back to the crowded room.

"There you are," said the boy with glasses. Paulina looked away. "Where have you been?" the boy said, leaning toward her.

"I have a boyfriend," Paulina said dispassionately.

"The other night—" the boy began.

"That was then, this is now," she said with exasperation. The boy's eyes squinted as if in pain, then he turned and left. Sadie and Allison immediately filled his place. Sadie put her hand behind Paulina's back and they danced very close together. Paulina silently forgave Sadie for the boots. She liked the way Allison danced, like a toy with dying batteries.

Apollo pulled his bandanna over his eyes and danced recklessly around the Venus Flytrap, humping air. A joint was passed around, burning those who danced into it. The forgotten eighties song came on again, the synthesizer stirring up feelings, and everyone screamed the sound of youth loving youth. Everyone was inside the same big mood.

Suddenly Tim was on the dance floor and Paulina saw only him. She pushed through people until she reached him. They danced entangled for a few songs—his hands on her breasts. The song sang to her. The semester had been slow, excruciating foreplay. Paulina pushed Tim against a wall. Everyone cheered and danced while she knelt before him, unzipping his fly.

It felt wrong to watch, but Fran watched. "That's the girl who slept with Gretchen's boyfriend," Angel told Fran. "She's going on the Norway trip." A police car drove past, and Tim's erection shone in the light, then it went dark again. Sadie and Allison fell into each other laughing.

The dancing became more flamboyant. Girls draped themselves on each other, and shook each other off. Straight boys danced carelessly with the Color Club boys. Then Cassie broke through the crowd and dragged Tim away. Her face was red from crying. Paulina stood flushed, wavering, then strode out the front door. She listened excitedly while Cassie told off Tim in the middle of the street. Cassie wouldn't accept his apology. She spit on his shoes and ran back to the party.

Paulina and Tim walked down the street, but Tim kicked rocks and wouldn't look at her. "Let's just go to your place and finish this," Paulina said, annoyed.

"We can't go to my place. I live with her. Let's go to your place," he said and looked at her with a sort of hatred. All her feelings of affection for him melted away and were replaced by stronger feelings of desperation and lust. She thought of Julian, asleep in her bed.

"Fuck it, how about here?" she said, motioning to an alley full of trash bins.

"Can't we use your place? I won't stay over or anything." They were almost to her place anyway. They walked without looking at each other. Paulina matched her steps to his, then consciously unmatched them. Once or twice she'd kissed someone at a party while Julian was in the other room, but she'd never had another guy in the apartment while he slept.

"Yeah, okay," she said. "My place."

He nodded. She tried to picture how it could work.

"That mopey dude won't be there, right?"

"He's a heavy sleeper," she said, her cruel laugh echoing through the night, surprising her.

In the laundry room of her apartment building, a half-finished painting leaned against the wall, depicting one of the girls upstairs with a mermaid tail. Tim nudged the painting toward him, revealing a smaller canvas behind it—a fish with peace-sign eyes. "With art like this, who needs art?" Paulina said, throwing her coat on the floor. Tim just looked at it. They kissed clumsily, stubbornly remembering what they had wanted before.

There was a barren feel to the basement, like it hadn't been made by humans. Paulina pulled her neighbor's laundry from the dryer and threw them on top of her coat. "I thought they'd be warm," Tim said as they climbed on the cold pile of sheets. His body held none of the qualities she'd expected of it. His torso had no drama. Languidly, without purpose, and then quicker once their bodies caught on, they worked on and finished what she had begun to think of as her Degree Project. Her orgasm was like a shooting star one pretends to have seen after a friend ecstatically points it out.

2

There were twelve students on the ten-day trip, along with an expert on Nordic history; Sampson Harris, the head of the Painting Department; and Nils, the painting grad who hung by Sampson's side. Tim's name on the signup list had been Paulina's incentive to sign her own, so she was wounded when she couldn't find him in the airport van. Paulina glumly surveyed those around her: Illustration majors and others whose majors were meaningless to guess. She spoke only once on the ride to the airport, loudly interrupting a discussion about a blind illustration teacher. "There is another van, correct?"

"Yessir," said Sampson Harris (late forties, portly, and beaming). Paulina disliked him. When Sampson gave a crit, his forehead wrinkled in thought, his eyes twinkled with self-love. His bravado and pride were typical of male painters. Male painters weren't self-deprecating like male illustrators. God, did she hate anything self-deprecating. Male painters weren't neat like male architects—but then neatness also annoyed her. And male sculptors thought themselves sensual (if clay) or brave (if metal).

Her opinion of Tim had worsened the night of the party, but in the days since then it had buoyed back up. All semester she'd clung to the idea of him. The laundry room was the only time they'd ever had sex, but this event had been christened and bedazzled in her memory until it bore little resemblance to what had taken place. Tim is in the other van, she told herself and sat back, letting the talk fade around her while she imagined herself and Tim, naked in a hotel suite, stoned, glamorous, inseparable.

But the airport was Tim-less. "His girlfriend made him cancel," an illustration major told her with unconcealed enjoyment. Paulina examined the others at the airport, people who didn't go to the art school. Stubby little families huddled near the TV monitors. Brain-dead teens wandered in toxic groups of two. Forgotten children sat like sentinels on top of mounds of luggage.

Paulina stood in despair, scrutinizing the pattern on the carpet, which stretched for miles. An unstable mind had created the pattern; Paulina assumed the designer had or would soon end his or her life. Paulina ran her boarding pass over her lips. She eyed a swarm of graphic designers and illustration majors, fearing they would try and befriend her. One of them, Marissa, was either the clueless graphic designer Paulina had met the week before or a girl so similarly flawed that the two might as well have teamed up and become one. Paulina noticed a gay freak from the Textiles Department whom she'd never felt akin to. Nervously, she took the little gray piece of cloth she carried in her bra and rubbed it against her lips. Her breasts were sweating in a tight shirt from eBay that didn't fit her.

When Paulina awoke that morning, she'd felt her life was an invitation to an even better life—she saw her name in wondrous script—but now she found herself in a social nightmare of unending duration. She decided to take a taxi back to school and surprise Sadie and Allison at Thai Dream or wherever they were spending break. She gathered her things. She would just tell Sampson and leave.

The college town seemed suddenly like the most boring, lacking place she'd ever been. She turned and saw Fran. A hive broke out on Paulina's neck. She clutched the scrap of blanket. She could entertain herself with Fran, even if she didn't befriend her, even though Paulina knew Fran was friends with a distraught design major who regularly shunned Paulina before Paulina had a chance to shun her first. She could hang out near Fran, and the others would assume they were friends and stay away from her.

Paulina found herself walking toward Fran, who was sitting on a bulky piece of luggage, her nail-bitten fingers skating over the stickers on her old Discman. She took off her headphones when Paulina approached her. Tiny voices sang from the headphones. A mindless beat beat on unhindered. After an unnecessary introduction, Paulina was entertained to hear Fran had a slight lisp. Paulina waited for Fran to draw her out in conversation, but Fran just smiled. Paulina stood paralyzed, snapping and unsnapping her hair clip. She looked for Nils, whose age gave him a slight edge over the others, but he was with Sampson.

Boarding the plane, Paulina stayed by Fran, conscious to seem apart. But the stale smell and muted colors inside the plane induced another anxiety in Paulina—a fear of boredom. She had barely spoken all day long, but now she found herself bargaining with the man and woman assigned to sit next to Fran, burying her aggression under a manipulative veneer of weakness and manners. Eventually the man in the window seat agreed and took Paulina's seat instead. Though she'd gotten her wish, Paulina sighed when she sat down and was careful not to look at Fran.

During takeoff, the girls stared silently out the window. The woman next to Fran slept. The white noise of the plane was disconcerting, then distracting, then comforting. After a few stray remarks, Paulina and Fran gradually found their common ground—the others on the trip, scattered in different seats on the plane. "I see James's work, clothes, and attitude as a protective measure against the flamboyance prevalent at our school," Paulina declared.

Fran found Paulina compelling and strange. After speaking her first words to Paulina at the gate, Fran felt sized up and then accepted. Fran had known they'd sit next to each other, and envisioned them, as if in a crystal ball, paired up to the exclusion of the other girls on the trip.

"My favorite," Fran said, motioning to Milo. Milo was the only male textiles major. He was skinny and friends with girl nerds. His art was draping fabrics. He had never kissed a boy (or girl) and lived in his gayness like a prison. "You will find someone, Milo, soon!" insisted his girlfriends, some of whom had never experienced such delight before—the delight of calling this stooped, eccentric creature their friend. "Milo is the watered-down version of some queers I knew in high school," Paulina said, but Fran sensed this wasn't true.

Very quickly, the girls formed a familiarity. Gretchen hated Paulina, Fran knew, but Gretchen felt far away. Paulina leaned her seat back and Fran could hear the muffled protest of the person behind her.

"What do you think those suckers are doing back home?" Paulina asked.

"Being with their families."

"What would you regret if we died right now in a crash?" Paulina asked.

Fran looked far into the fabric of the seat in front of her. "I guess I don't have enough good paintings for a solid 'in memoriam' show," she said. "But it doesn't really matter."

"It doesn't," Paulina said and laughed. "Do you have a boyfriend?" she asked.

Fran thought instantly of Marvin, but Marvin was not her boyfriend in any sense. "Do you?" she asked.

Paulina stared into the dark window of the plane. "Yeah, but I'm ending it."

"Who?" Fran asked, with increasing curiosity.

Paulina leaned over and took out a sleep mask from her big leather purse. She pulled the mask on top of her forehead, matting down her curls. "I believe his name is Julian," Paulina said flatly.

"Is he printmaking?" asked Fran.

"Film, but I've never seen anything he's made."

"I think I had a class with him once, an art history lecture. Does he have long, scraggly hair?"

"I cut it," Paulina said in the same emotionless way. She slid her sleep mask over her eyes and said nothing for several hours.

In any foreign country, Paulina wanted to belong. She lagged a block behind the group. They trudged along, stopping at every museum in sight. They ate lunches on picnic tables, the boys all speaking their bad Norwegian. With disdain, Paulina watched as their accents spawned stupid personas. James was the worst offender. His persona had its own name, Gulltopp, the name of the poor man he'd sat next to on the plane. James's Gulltopp did a funny dance before and after meals and spoke only about fjords.

In a tragic use of alphabetical order, Paulina was sentenced to room with Marissa, who spoke her thoughts freely and often, injuring Paulina with her exaggerated wonder. The first night, Marissa gushed about Norway, and Europe, the artists of the past, while Paulina listened to her earplugs expand. Paulina believed that only Fran deserved to be her friend. Fran, who sat hunched against the wall during art history lectures, who stared too long at birds and bugs and faraway noises, who played with her hair so incessantly that Paulina knew she would never pass a job interview.

In a room of tapestries at the National Museum of Art, Paulina told Fran, "I need to sleep with someone exciting."

"Ooh, like Nils?"

Paulina made a face. "No, like a fucking Viking from the past."

Fran laughed, avoiding the glance of the other person in the room, an old man clutching a cane. The tapestries were all

Viking scenes—tall ships slanting on the water, a sword fight inside a treasure cave. The details hurt Fran's head if she examined them too closely. Neat narrow lines indicated light and shadow. The texture of the waves stood in stark contrast to the clouds, to the sails, the glint of the swords, the hair curling out of helmets. "We could find someone like that," she said.

"Someone who holds a whole chicken in one hand and eats from it," said Paulina.

"And he's got long, blond hair."

"Yeah he does. His dick is enormous—"

"Not enormous, but a good size, and of good texture," said Fran.

"Snakeskin?" said Paulina.

"Velvet," said Fran. The old man left, and they were alone for the first time. "How is his house decorated?"

"With a single zebra-skin rug," Paulina said, staring with unfocused eyes. "What is his name?"

"Blood Axe," said Fran, reading the card on the wall.

Paulina laughed. "Perfect."

"And he's followed by a pack of animals," said Fran.

"He can take five puppies in his hand and squeeze them into a full-sized dog."

"His native tongue can't pronounce our names."

"Or his own name!" Paulina said.

"He's killed men, but never a woman," Fran added.

"His torso has a lot of drama."

"What kind of drama?" asked Fran.

"Like scars and hair and muscles and things."

"Does he carry a bloody ax?" Fran asked.

"Not these days. But once he did," Paulina said wistfully. They laughed.

They strolled out of the museum and into the chilly air. They huddled for warmth. They lost the group. They posed with statues. They found their way.

Norway was magnificent. Train rides along the fjords gave them clear views of vast, overphotographed glaciers. Though Paulina refused to mix, the others formed experimental social groups, sparked by an ambiguity as to who was cool. The students wandered around Oslo, clueless and buzzed. They had solemn moments in Norwegian history museums, face-to-face with an ancient gown or worn-down coin.

Freed from Sadie and Allison, Paulina spent the long bus rides breaking down their personality flaws for Fran's entertainment. Sadie was always bragging about her healthy and natural lifestyle choices—drinking only on weekends, never eating fried foods—but went to the tanning booths *weekly*, saying she had an "appointment downtown," and was always drenched in perfume. Sadie loved pictures of cats and dogs but not the creatures themselves. She was always scolding Paulina for not recycling, as if she understood the earth's innermost perils. Paulina declared her incapable of intellectual thought.

As for Allison, she had the bored look of a stranger on a bus, even when she was listening attentively. She took herself so seriously as an artist that Paulina felt embarrassed for her. She often had pimples and took no time to disguise them. The biggest problem was Allison's hair, which had neither the articulation of curls nor the sleekness of straight hair and was thick, like unprocessed wool.

Paulina described the tedium of Julian, how he slumped around her apartment, oblivious to her other lovers. She criticized all the dull lovers of their school, and the pretention rampant among the art history majors.

"There's an art history major?" Fran asked.

Paulina nodded. "It's new." After finding art making meaningless, Paulina had begged the registrar to count her art history credits toward a major, eventually seducing him. During each of their nights together, she had discussed the benefits of an art history major so casually that even after her successful academic petition he believed that they'd thought of the idea together.

After the first night of the trip, Paulina had convinced Fran's roommate, Angel, to trade rooms with her so that Paulina and Fran could room together. Fran noticed Paulina rubbing the little gray rag on her lips at night, but she didn't ask about it. Fran understood that being this close with Paulina had its restrictions. She couldn't visibly socialize with the others on the trip, though everyone was very nice and always inviting her to hang out. Being with Paulina was like being under Soviet rule, she thought during a few outrageous moments, but it was worth it.

At a dance club in Bergen, Paulina and Fran experienced the same fathomless fun they felt at the Color Club. Each moment they amazed themselves. In dancing they spread themselves and saw themselves in the reaction of those around them. We must be very beautiful to feel this beautiful, Fran thought. The pleasant shock of a new country made them feel they deserved it, that the earth swiveled to show them things. They drank and flirted with skinny Norwegian boys. They spent so much time together without getting sick of each other, it was inspiring.

Paulina no longer needed Sadie or Allison. She envisioned herself and Fran socially dominating their small school. In good colors, far in the future, she imagined them growing even more sophisticated and successful. In lives abundant with luck and love. In LA or Paris. In short leather jackets.

While Paulina deep conditioned her hair, Fran drank beers with James, Angel, and Marissa at a bar close to their hotel in Stavanger.

"Why do you hang out with that crazy bitch?" asked James. "You should hang out with us." The others nodded in agreement.

"She is dangerous and unpredictable," Marissa hissed.

"Ask her about her semester at Smith sometime," Angel said.

"Smith?" James asked.

"Paulina was a big lesbo at Smith," Angel said. "She seduced every girl there, then got kicked out." Just when it seemed like Paulina could not be more interesting to Fran, something like this would emerge.

"Every girl?" James asked.

"Practically. I'm serious. At least half of them. She told me about it when she transferred here."

"You roomed with her?" Marissa asked.

"One semester. I have never met anyone with a higher opinion of herself. I had to convince her that she didn't deserve to use both closets. That I needed a closet too, even if my clothes weren't as special as hers."

Fran was used to hearing Paulina criticized. Freshman year, Paulina had seduced Gretchen's high school boyfriend visiting from Northwestern. He'd gone to a party while Gretchen hot glued cardboard for her foundation class. The boyfriend fell for Paulina, but Paulina refused to talk to him afterward. The boyfriend broke up with Gretchen, who was devastated and then obsessed. Vital parts of Gretchen had been destroyed, and she knew it, but couldn't repair herself.

"Oh my god," Angel said, "look." A few feet away, Nils was flirting with the bartender, a woman with blond hair and horse teeth.

"Do you think he's cute? I think he's so cute," Angel said. Nils took out a pencil and started to draw the waitress in his sketchbook.

Fran shrugged. Generally speaking, Paulina and Fran felt grad students to be egomaniacs who had charmed themselves into a stupor. At school, the grad students all had small cells where they played artist, sitting in a chair from SUPERTHRIFT mulling over their lives, experimenting uselessly with video (all of them!), reading online artist interviews. Their résumés hovered in their thoughts.

"They try too hard," Fran said. "Grad students, I mean."

Every grad student TA'd a class—sitting smugly in the back of the room, smoking theatrically outside the woodshop, talking too much about too many artists. Always the grad students were breaking up their long-distance relationships and partnering up with one another, fighting boredom with infatuation. Every year, there was one grad who rose above this—a girl who didn't just understand the undergrads, but could rule over them. An artist would show up and inject dye into a fish tank filled with hair gel, depicting the scene of Helen Keller and the water pump, or make a video that wasn't lo-fi and self-reflective, but instead brilliant.

Nils was tattooed. He was okay. In the hotel elevator he'd told Fran he liked her pheromones. The conversation veered from him to a grad Fran couldn't picture. She missed Paulina's cruel gaze. She tried to imagine the insults Paulina would whisper to her. Paulina might say Angel was a "daft beast with a big crease." She'd once called James a dildo with eyes.

A week into the trip, Angel had grown tired of Marissa and, by the time they got to Kristiansand, wanted to room with Fran again, like she'd been assigned. Angel made it clear that she couldn't stand Paulina, but Paulina refused to leave, and instead shared a bed with Fran in a "Nordic sleepover."

"I actually fantasize about Blood Axe," Paulina told Fran.

"You do not!"

"I do," said Paulina.

"So do I," Fran said.

"Who the hell is Blood Axe?" Angel asked from her bed.

"Just this guy we fucked," Paulina said.

The next day, back in Oslo with the afternoon free, Paulina wanted to get lost in Frogner Park and search for hallucino-genic mushrooms, but Fran wanted to go to an amusement park with Angel and Milo. "Just go," Paulina said dismissively. "It's not like we're connected by a cord or anything." At an Internet café, Paulina read an e-mail from Sadie, again about the boy she'd met on vacation, but more in-depth—his hobbies, his family history. Paulina skimmed it quickly, then composed her own reply.

Though she is the only bearable company in the country, I can't help but notice that Fran's inconsistent, adolescent wardrobe is a nostalgic circle jerk for the past. At 20 years old, she still remains challenged by simple tasks such as clear speaking.

"I got high last night and had revelations," Fran told Paulina the next morning.

Paulina snorted. She had spent the evening wandering around the city feeling lonely and boring. She'd refused to sleep in Fran's room or her own, and had ended up in Nils's room, rubbing against him while he talked about his girlfriend. It distressed her that he wouldn't sleep with her. She had missed Julian.

"Anything you do with those losers has nothing to do with me," Paulina said. It was their last day in Norway. The Viking Ship Museum was amazing, but it was wasted on them. They were sick of museums. They spent a good half hour deciding which boat could best support their weight, and then crawled inside it to hide, nibbling a chocolate Fran had bought on the street.

"What do you think Julian is doing right now?" asked Fran.

"Filming a bug and then squashing it," Paulina said.

"Do you love him?"

"Not really. For a while I liked having him around." Across the room, a female museum guard approached a male museum guard. "I spent a lot of time with him last semester. Showed him the ways of a woman, wasted time philosophizing. Tried to outfit him in better clothing, but he resisted." Paulina watched as the two guards conferred, then walked toward them.

"It's easy to dismiss things when they aren't nearby," Fran said, smoothing the worn wood of the ship.

"What?" Paulina said, feigning distraction. The guards approached Paulina and Fran. The man told them sternly in Norwegian to get off the ship, and then the female guard told them the same in overenunciated English. Fran blushed wildly as she disembarked, in a way Paulina found beautiful and idiotic.

The girls meandered around the museum, avoiding their classmates. Their classmates ruined the dream. "It's like traveling to the moon, only to see the junk you left on your bedroom floor," Paulina whispered.

They saw Nils doing an involved sketch of a ship and felt bad for him. "Do you think he's sexy?" Paulina asked Fran.

"He's okay," Fran said.

"Who do you really like?" Paulina said.

Fran wouldn't say.

"James? Tim? Dean? Troy? Zane?"

Fran smiled. "Dean, Troy, and Zane for sure."

"No, really though. Who do you want to sleep with? Whose little cock do you draw in the margins of your art history handouts?"

Fran hesitated. She liked keeping things to herself. She hadn't told Paulina that she'd kissed Nils after the play they'd seen in Bergen, or gotten a matching tattoo with Milo at the amusement park—a little pink ice-cream cone behind her ear.

"Stop being so precious!" Paulina scolded. The female guard glared at them. "She's been following us!" Paulina exclaimed.

"Marvin," Fran said impulsively.

Paulina laughed. "Everyone likes Marvin! He doesn't count."

"Not the way I do," Fran said. She'd deluded herself in believing she'd discovered him.

"He's beyond us anyway. He's like a gorgeous dog who paints," Paulina said. "He's untouchable."

"I'm going to touch him. No one has really tried," said Fran.

"You're unreal. Do you know how many times I've tried to seduce him?"

Fran looked at her with dismay. "You can't," she said.

"Are you kidding? You can't claim him. What makes your Marvin infatuation more important than mine?"

Fran's teeth locked. Marissa approached with something unwieldy she'd bought at the gift shop, but Paulina snapped at her and she retreated.

For the rest of the day, Paulina and Fran avoided each other. Fran walked the rolling fields of Vigeland Park with Milo and James. Paulina got drunk with Nils but he refused to let her sleep in his room. "You're a twenty-seven-year-old on a school trip!" Paulina told him. "I mostly just feel bad for you," she muttered as he closed the door. Then she walked sadly back to her assigned room with Marissa, fumbling with her card key, loudly undressing and humming to herself. Marissa struggled to maintain her composure while also pretending to sleep.

In the morning, everyone was packing for the airport when Paulina burst into a fury. "What did you do with them?" she yelled at Marissa.

"I don't know what you're talking about, freak! Stop screaming at me!" Marissa screamed.

Fran heard their voices from across the hall. "What is it?" she asked, walking into the room.

"She's hidden my hair potions!" Paulina said. "How low and immature!"

Fran started searching under Paulina's bed.

"What do they look like?" James asked, peeking in from the hallway. Angel joined him in the doorway, but neither helped to look.

"They're these glass jars. Sort of baby-food sized," Fran said.

Paulina had refused to tell Fran her ingredients, but the stuff worked. Paulina had put some in Fran's hair a few nights before, and for twenty-four hours Fran was invincible to humidity and frizz. Now, however, Paulina could only hold up the empty bag where she'd kept the bottles and rub her blanket to her lips.

"Wait, is that the thing you were telling me about?" James asked Marissa.

Paulina fumed.

Marissa nodded. "Her *blanket!*"

"It's a tattered rag," James said, "I'd hardly call it a blanket!"

Paulina glared at him, her whole body tense. "Shut up, losers! Marissa, what did you do with them?"

"Why would I move your hair goop?"

"As a passive-aggressive hate crime against me," Paulina insisted. Marissa laughed in disbelief.

"God, you've been such a bitch on this trip," James said. "You barely made eye contact with anyone."

"You deserve every bad thing that will happen to you!" Marissa yelled.

Paulina kicked over Marissa's suitcase and emptied her toiletry bag while Marissa berated her with an incoherent emotional speech.

In a low drawer beneath the sink, Fran found the bottles and thrust them at Paulina.

"What's that, lube?" James said, but Paulina was too busy putting the bottles in her bag to respond. She carefully put the bag in her suitcase. Her eyes glazed over as she held the blanket to her mouth.

"That girl's got a serious oral fixation," Angel said and James snickered.

"Joan of Arc had a blanket," Paulina said, but Fran knew this couldn't be true. Angel cracked up. Paulina glared at her, waiting for her to stop, but Angel laughed loudly while Paulina boiled beside her. Just when Fran thought the whole thing might subside and Angel was catching her breath and letting out little laughs of relief, Paulina leapt at Angel, and in one stunning movement, Angel grabbed Paulina's arm and flung her to the ground.

. . .

"Oh! I hate her so much it's murdering me," Paulina said, throwing herself on Fran's bed.

"Angel or Marissa?"

"I hate her hair, and her fucking day camp wardrobe. I hate when people do that—form a club of losers to torture you," Paulina said. "Marissa," she said. "Both," she said. She cast her angry eyes at Fran, who sat by the hotel room window watching the doorman smoke. "What do *you* hate?" she asked Fran. Fran said nothing. Paulina waited impatiently, eyeing the welt on her arm in the mirror. Her hair was unruly and she liked herself less because of it. She looked like a doll whose factory-made hair was not meant to be brushed but had been brushed violently.

"I hate when people call alcohol a 'social lubricant,'" Fran said.

On the flight back, Fran and Nils watched an action movie on the TV above their heads. Paulina sulked next to a stranger. In the van back to school, when everyone sang along to "Bohemian Rhapsody," Paulina just stiffened.

Back on the ordinary streets of their little college town, Fran felt that childhood feeling, that the world was shrinking down to normal after stretching out before her. She and Paulina passed the pizza place where the employees were brats, where she and Gretchen used to eat dinner after 3-D Design. On Ridge Street, she turned toward Wilson Street, but Paulina grabbed her sleeve. "I'm down this way," Paulina said, pointing down Ridge.

"Oh, this is where we say good-bye and are never friends again," Fran said.

They laughed and embraced, Paulina's breasts pushing against Fran's.

3

Julian and Paulina walked to the thin canal that cut through town. Swans made it seem special. A huge mall rose in the distance, but they walked toward an abandoned area of grass. Julian hummed a few notes from an Ennio Morricone score, quietly so Paulina wouldn't hear. Then louder, so she would. It excited him to be around her. Her moods were so erratic. He could not control her. He looked at the deformed shadow she cast in the grass and smiled. He looked at his own shadow, expecting it to be noble, but it too was foreshortened and grotesque.

Behind the rusted shell of a school bus, they lowered themselves to the ground and pulled off each other's clothing. The grass poked and itched them. Watching Julian kiss her pale breasts, Paulina felt like an empress, one who didn't protect her people. Julian pushed his pants down and she guided him into her. She felt nailed to the universe, in the spell that made things work. They both moved at the same time. They were impatient. There was no rhythm. The irrelevant voice of a child floated across the canal like a runaway balloon. They stopped.

"You go," Paulina said, trying to stay graceful. Julian moved back and forth like a swimmer. Paulina felt she would never reach her orgasm, that it was continents away and unknown to her. A train hooted in the distance. She got on her hands and knees. "Like this, so you can . . ." They did it that way for a while and Paulina sensed the orgasm and strove to meet it. She grabbed her breast and imagined it was someone's. Her orgasm was drowned out by his.

Julian lay back on the grass, caught his breath, and kissed Paulina. She scrunched away from him. He kissed her again.

"I don't want to date you anymore," Paulina told him.

"You love me," he said.

"Nah, not really. Not lately."

"What am I, your discarded plaything?"

Paulina felt his semen pool in her underwear. She had wanted one last time. As she'd told Sadie more than once, "Brains can fuck."

The breakup sex reminded her of her semester at Smith. That had all started with Sally in the yoga shack by the lake. But Paulina couldn't avoid her feelings for Audrey, who gazed at Paulina unabashedly in the dining hall, forcing Paulina to eat in a rugged, macho way to impress her. Then, in a steamy room at the Smith botanical gardens, she felt up Susan Bradley, a girl preoccupied with sustainable living. Later, in her dorm room, a knock.

The girls at Smith had been naturally drawn to Paulina, whose critical gaze held weight. She followed each loaded stare to its giggling, passionate realization. But, by midterms, the girls revolted, led by Audrey. Sally looked on, stunned out of her heartbreak, as one of them punched Paulina in the face. The girl's fake sapphire ring left a scar. After, Paulina tried to punish the girls by seducing the male teachers they all lauded. Only one was weak to this, and he was the worst looking of all. The scandal led to Paulina's transfer.

"Did you stray from me on your trip?" Julian asked. His choice of words, his measured speech, his expression of defeat annoyed Paulina. He took everything too seriously. He silently buttoned, zipped, and belted his pants. "Was it James?" he asked glumly.

"God, no!"

"Nils?" he asked incredulously.

Paulina was ashamed that she hadn't slept with anyone on the trip. It was unlike her. Fran had kept her occupied. She scratched hard at a trapped hair on her leg, while her lips quivered into a smile.

"I didn't want to tell you," said Paulina, "but me and Fran," she paused thoughtfully, "I mean Fran and I met . . ."

She laughed. "You are never going to believe this, but we met this huge Viking named Blood Axe."

"Shut up," Julian said with disgust.

"No, really. I mean, it's possible it's not his real name, but we met this huge hulking guy and were swept away. Fran lost her virginity to him, to Blood Axe," she said. "On his zebra-skin rug." Julian stared at the water, looking hurt. "Don't tell her I told you," Paulina said. "Really, I wasn't going to say anything, because I knew you wouldn't believe me. And you know me, I wanted to be good, but it promised to be such a unique experience."

"Bullshit," Julian said.

"It's how I got this," she said, showing him the black-and-blue mark on her arm. "He's unaware of his own strength," she said, as if defending him. Paulina's face was stoic, while inside she felt glee.

Julian cringed. "You weren't going to tell me?" He examined her coldly.

"We've been drifting apart for some time," Paulina said. "Blood Axe just sealed the deal."

"Which one is Fran?" Julian asked. "Curly hair?"

"Yeah," said Paulina. "Nice girl."

"She's a virgin?"

"Not anymore."

Julian sighed. "Leave it to you to find some—"

"Viking," she interrupted.

"Viking poser."

"Like I said, a Viking. From long ago. He was divine. I don't expect you to understand."

"Fuck off," Julian said and left Paulina in the grass.

She felt a stab of longing as he grew smaller and smaller in her sight and wished he'd turn around and walk her home. Even if he just wanted to fight about it some, Paulina would have fought some. She tried to salvage the glee, but now there were only a few glittery bits that dissipated once she noticed them.

The Junior Painting Studio was a large room divided by white drywall partitions. Students worked late nights in their studios and idolized the artists of the past, especially the lesser-known ones—Dubuffet, Guston, even Morandi and his underwhelming little vases and bowls. The painters glued pennies and trash and family heirlooms on to their paintings. They painted their friends making out with old television stars. They painted their friends nude in the streetlight. Nude at the Pyramids. They thought of a concept and created a series exhausting the concept.

Some of the studios were clean, like a gallery showing work. Others, like Fran's, were stuffed like a locker with clothes, books, broken mirrors, pill bottles, doll heads, candy wrappers, stiff brushes, old glue, and stray stretcher bars. Her paintings were thought to be strong—she'd been compared to Elizabeth Peyton and Bonnard—but she didn't work as hard as the others. She was slow and took breaks. Spring semester, her studio was across from Marvin's. *Other love has felt normal, but my love for Marvin feels like a wilderness,* Fran wrote in the margin of her art history handout. *I don't just love him. I like everything he does. Everything he touches seems lucky. It is painful to watch him.*

She drifted toward him naturally, like a dog. He seemed to like her, but had never asked her to do anything, even go to the cafeteria. People were perturbed by Marvin, who had no definite social allegiance and would cruise into a party, then leave wordlessly. He didn't need anything from anyone. Once, in the computer lab, Fran clicked on a file saved to the desktop and read an artist statement: *My work affects my relationships with people. Sometimes a painting will change my relationship to my parents, even though the painting is completely abstract and mostly one color with some texture.* There was no name on the document, but Fran felt drawn to whoever wrote it, and was sure it was Marvin.

It was Fran's first time in studio since break. She watched Marvin while she stretched a canvas. He sat on the floor dipping acorns in paint.

"Why acorns?" James asked.

"I thought the mice would eat them," he said, "but they didn't." Mice had moved in over the winter and lived in the mess the painters made, eating crumbs and construction paper.

"Why that color?" James asked as he walked by.

"I have a lot of it," Marvin said. His curly hair was in a mess over his eyes. "How was Norway, Fran?" he asked. Their eyes met for the third time that day.

"Pretty," she said, and her body warmed like she was talking to God.

"You could never date a boy like that, who lives without needing to know himself," Gretchen told Fran, but Gretchen knew nothing. The girls walked out of the studios without looking at each other. Both wore patchwork backpacks they'd bought at the hippie store freshman year.

Fran and Gretchen had become friends in Foundation Drawing one day after Gretchen's hair elastic flew through the air, narrowly missing the model. Gretchen was understated. No hairdo announced her. She was a graphic design major, which Fran found uninspiring. Gretchen wasn't free like the others. She danced, drank, and drew, but never gave herself over to it. She never felt the light of everyone's eyes upon her; nor did she crave this kind of light.

"He talks in a baby voice," Gretchen said.

"No, he doesn't. He just isn't listening to how he sounds."

"You know you didn't call me back," Gretchen said.

"I know. I'm sorry. I had so much to catch up on."

"How was the trip anyway? Did you socialize with the enemy?"

"Who?" said Fran. "Oh, I mean, in passing."

At the lecture, Fran and Gretchen watched a successful New York artist strip to her underwear and gnaw on a man-sized piece of chocolate. During the Q&A, students asked embarrassing questions and name-dropped other artists. The questions were met with a collective groan, as if the student body were one body, one that couldn't accept itself. After, the artist put a curse on them, insisting: "Only one person in this room will make it in the art world."

It took a lifetime to walk to SUPERTHRIFT, and much of it was highway. Normally Sadie drove, but she had lent Eileen her car. Skipping ahead of Sadie and Allison, Paulina exclaimed, "I am free! I can fuck anyone I want! I can do as I please!"

"But you were doing that before," Sadie said.

"But this time with the clearest of minds! An available bed, and a purely selfish heart. The things I will accomplish," she whispered loudly.

"What are you going to accomplish?" Allison asked dubiously.

Paulina stopped walking. "Hey! Lay off," she said.

After a step, Sadie and Allison stopped too. Paulina eyed them suspiciously. "What happened here while I was gone, anyway? Did the gap close further without me?"

"What gap?" Sadie asked, though she knew. They resumed walking.

"Those precious inches between your ass and hers. What did I miss around here anyway? Anything revolutionary?"

"There was a flood at the Feminist Warehouse," Sadie said.

"That guy Fluff sold Eileen cocaine that was laced with something."

"Oh, and my boyfriend visited and Allison met him," said Sadie.

"He's great," Allison said. They smiled.

"What? What boyfriend?" Paulina asked. Cars sped by like bullets.

"Eric," Sadie said emphatically. "Remember? I told you about him before you left and I wrote those e-mails."

"Oh, yeah," Paulina said. She didn't want Sadie to have a boyfriend because she didn't want to have to listen to her talk about him. But at least he didn't live there; at least Paulina didn't have to see him. "I'm sure he's great," Paulina said. The shoulder narrowed and they walked on in single file: Sadie, then Allison, then Paulina. Paulina's head filled with images of lame boyfriends, ones who wore puka-shell necklaces, Adidas running pants, and shirts with words.

. . .

At SUPERTHRIFT, remnants from hundreds of dull lives hung before them on plastic hangers. Even when the girls found something remarkable, it always seemed like the original owner had misunderstood and squandered it. Every nightgown came with a few bad dreams. This depressive air empowered the girls. Their lives were incredible! When the clothes fit, they felt they'd looted the lame, the poor, and the dead. When they didn't, the girls dismissed used clothing as gross.

Besides the clothes, they searched earnestly in the cassette pile, the furniture, the shoe racks. Everything seemed like something they could improve, that no one yet had known how to improve. Allison bought the paintings—amateur still lifes and common landscapes, tacky beach scenes with sponged-on clouds, clown paintings, sadly confident bubble-lettered names—to gesso over in her studio.

Paulina began a methodical search in Blouses, though she never had luck there. She listened to Sadie and Allison in Skirts, one aisle over. Their voices rose and fell. They were either trashing Eileen's work or praising it. Paulina lingered a while, wondering, before marching off into Evening Dresses. At first nothing appealed to her. She closed herself off to every option without really considering them. Most of the dresses she'd seen before. Some had sweat or deodorant marks. Many had no inner life.

The song changed, reminding Paulina that she was free of Julian, and she loosened up. A few items intrigued her and she took some chances, ignoring any indication of size—it'll stretch, she thought, or I'll cut it. Once her arm was weighed down with clothes, she walked triumphantly to the dressing rooms.

"Goin' in, girls!" she yelled to Sadie and Allison, but heard no reply. She waited, then smiled, knowing they would scamper over. When Paulina found something that flattered her, Allison and Sadie always hovered around to admire her while she pranced in the aisle in front of her dressing room. Sadie had long given up debating—anything Paulina found "fabulous," Sadie praised as well. But Paulina didn't just want their approval; she wanted them to be jealous.

Paulina hung her fur coat on a hook, wincing when the bottom grazed the disgusting dressing room floor. She took off her shirt and pants and piled them on top of her shoes in the corner. It would be nasty to have sex in a SUPERTHRIFT dressing room, but she'd have liked to be able to say she'd done it.

The first dress was huge and Paulina flung it on the floor. She'd found a nice pair of pants, but before she got too excited she spotted a bloodstain on the butt and extracted herself from the situation. "Sadie!" she called. "Allison!" She wanted to tell them about the bloodstain and show them the jumper she was about to try on: a blue-gray cotton thing that narrowed into shorts. It was the kind of outfit one wore spontaneously, she felt. When she put it on, her breasts swelled out the top. Wearing it, she felt like a provocative babysitter. With the jumper came the promise of warm weather and new love.

She got very close to the mirror trying to discern the pattern on the fabric. Sailboats? Flowers? Nope. Paisley! Allison and Sadie still hadn't appeared. What are they doing, she thought, fucking on a used mattress? Until that moment, the thought of anything sexual between them had never occurred to her. She frowned at the idea and made the "gross" face.

All day, Sadie and Allison had seemed distant. Upon first greeting Paulina, Sadie had made a snide remark about Farm Girl Fashion Disaster, and though it sounded familiar, it took Paulina a moment to decode. They're jealous, she thought to herself posing in the mirror. She remembered fondly how her old dog, Mildred, had gone crazy with jealousy whenever Paulina had the smell of another dog on her. Maybe she hadn't fully accounted for the amount of time Julian had taken away from them. Well, whatever, she thought, a girl couldn't always be with Sadie and Allison or she'd perish! She smiled at herself in the jumper, *so cute*.

Where were they? She called out to them again. The jumper

began to look silly in the mirror. *Sadie wouldn't approve, would make fun of the jumper.* Also, it was way too tight. It clamped around her stomach and pinched under her arms.

Then she realized—it was a child's jumper. Her face flushed. She felt hugely stupid. *Sadie will burst out laughing at this, yes, uncontrollably. Allison too.* She tried to shimmy out of it, but it shrunk with every movement.

"Yes, what?" asked Sadie finally. Paulina saw her through the gap where the curtain failed to meet the wall.

"Oh, nothing. I had it on, but nothing now."

"Let me see," Allison said.

"No, I don't need any opinions," Paulina said, still imprisoned in the jumper. It looked like a doll's apron. Sadie poked the curtain. Paulina hastily pulled it shut.

"Chill, girl," Sadie said. She poked the curtain with her elbow and Paulina flinched.

"We found a lot of good things," Allison said.

"Where?!" Paulina asked. Defeated, she stopped struggling and stood before the mirror, one arm in and one out. Her hair had looked ideal when she left for SUPERTHRIFT, but all order had been destroyed by the wind. Her life felt like a mistake. She looked and felt like a shipwrecked alien whose mission had gotten horribly derailed.

Art school had been an impulsive decision. Paulina hadn't really thought she'd get in. Her portfolio was mostly doodles she'd drawn over the photos in her high school yearbook. When she showed up, she found that the other students knew much more about art history than she did. They drew better. They worked harder. After a week, she abandoned her artistic goals. It was preposterous to have "artistic goals." She cringed at the very words.

Then she'd seen the Venus Flytrap crack up an entire party with her exceptional laugh. Wearing only a cardboard head-dress and Troy's boxer briefs, the Venus Flytrap danced with total abandon. She trembled and shook, sacrificing her body to the song, letting it fill with spirits. Paulina envied the performance. She decided her personality would be her art and revamped her closet with SUPERTHRIFT treasures. She overheard the disturbing life story of a deranged man downtown and adopted it as her own.

Paulina's ass hurt from sitting on the tiny corner seat in her dressing room. With concentration, she finally managed to take off the jumper without ripping it too badly. Then, slowly, she put her clothes back on, as if her existence were futureless and blank, and dressing just an automatic, ceremonial act of the life she'd left behind. She listened to Allison and Sadie try on their finds.

"Oh my god, those pants rule!" Sadie told Allison.

"You think? I feel like a tightrope walker or someone," Allison said.

"Check it out, Paulina," Sadie called, but Paulina refused to view their successes.

While the two of them paid, Paulina moped in the parking lot. She missed Fran, and the feeling was unique, as Paulina made it a rule to miss no one. When Sadie and Allison came out, they barely acknowledged her and continued their conversation. This stung Paulina, but she followed after them, pretending she was an alien sent to study Sadie and Allison's feeble minds. She thought, *My findings are quite abysmal, Rolan, ruler of Rolanzil. Their preening techniques are surprisingly rudimentary. Especially the tall one, whose tresses hang off her head like dead grasses.*

"You'll be there, right, Paulina?" Sadie asked nonchalantly, like the three had been talking all along.

"Where?" Paulina asked bitterly.

"My apparel show!"

"If I'm alive," Paulina said, clutching her fur as if it could leave her.

4

Julian sat in movie theaters long after the credits. He slumped around the cafeteria. He'd begun school with friends, until one day he realized it was easier to see movies without inviting anyone along, and this turned him into a loner. He completed his assignments mechanically, and the films were dim and infuriating. A salt pile growing and melting. A glove wandering through the grass. When his classmates discussed his work, he could hear the clock ticking on the wall.

In the library, Julian spied on Paulina and Fran, wondering what was between them. He imagined Blood Axe, muscular and blond, Fran, naked and shivering on a zebra-skin rug, and Paulina, bathing in a claw-footed tub, all of them lounging in a log cabin with crude quilts and knitted things nailed to the walls. At first the story hadn't made sense, but with every step away from Paulina he'd begun to accept it. Of course it made him nauseous to imagine her with Blood Axe, but almost immediately his mind found refuge in Fran. Just a semester or two before, he had been a virgin too, before Paulina took him home.

The library was a maze of bookcases and parquet floors. Big windows were covered with dusty velvet curtains. There were few people in the library. Students were clicking away in the computer labs, wasting their eyes in the white light, while the library creaked on without them. A library is like a sunken ship, thought Julian. It doesn't change as the world changes.

He walked down the aisle toward Paulina and Fran, scanning the stacks. He took a big book from the shelf and pretended to read it.

"Hey, Brains," Paulina said brightly.

He turned as if surprised. "Julian," he said, and extended his hand to Fran. Before the breakup, he'd never thought of Fran, but now saw she had her own peculiar beauty. She wore a long knit skirt and a Little League jersey. Between buttons, Julian could see a swatch of her bra and a small triangle of pale skin.

"I know who you are," Fran said.

Julian leaned against the stacks.

"Your reputation precedes you, Fran," he said, looking to her face for a reaction.

"I don't have a reputation," Fran said laughing.

"Really, she doesn't," Paulina said plainly.

"How are things?" he asked.

"Thingy," said Paulina.

Fran studied him. He was holding a book on ancient casting techniques. There was something in his voice, something he had taken from Paulina, or something Paulina had gotten from him. Though Paulina had dismissed him, at some point she had chosen him for herself. Fran tried to see him this way, in Paulina's high opinion.

Julian slid the book back into the stacks, stretching this motion out to draw their attention.

"What's my reputation?" Fran asked. Paulina sighed loudly.

"That you don't refuse an adventure," Julian said. Fran laughed, but Paulina turned away as if to leave.

"Until we meet again," he said, like the heroes of old movies the girls had never seen. Then he was off, ducking out the door, anticipating with pleasure the certainty that they would discuss him. Again, he imagined Fran in Blood Axe's cabin. There was something peaceful about her nervousness.

"So corny! God," Paulina said. A boy glared at them. The girls moved to another row and sat down. They often hung out at the library before their sociology class, lingering in the most boring stacks where they could talk freely. To the girls, a library was a dignified place. Like a graveyard, it made one feel very alive.

"Have you seen him since the river?" Fran asked.

"He's obsessed with me!" Paulina said. She had no idea where he'd been before the library or where he'd go after. It unnerved her.

"I keep thinking about the river!" Fran whispered.

"I think a family saw us," Paulina said, reliving it.

When Fran went to the Painting Building that weekend, Marvin was the only one there, crouched in James's studio. "Look at these mouse babies," he said and held one out to Fran. The captive mouse scratched at Marvin's fingers. Light shone through its pink, round ears.

"Oh, wow!" Fran exclaimed. Marvin put the mouse in the fishbowl where he kept his colored pencils.

"I was going to dip their feet in paint and have them run around on the canvas," he said. "But first, I wanna put costumes on them."

"I have costumes for them!" Fran said, rushing to her studio. "Last semester I got these kids' gloves with *Wizard of Oz* finger puppets." She dug in a box of corroded paint tubes. Marvin caught another mouse.

"If you can't find them, I have pipe cleaners," he said. Fran threw aside some sketches she'd done of the Norway trip. One of them had her and Paulina dancing on top of a cake. She hadn't realized its lesbian undertone until her classmates happily pointed it out in crit. I was just being surreal, she told them again in her head.

"Found them!" Each finger of the glove was a different character. The Dorothy finger had little braids of yarn. The Tin Man had a shimmery metallic hat.

"These are perfect," Marvin said. They went to his studio and cut the fingers off the gloves and the tops off each finger. "It's like a tube top," he said, forcing a costume on each squirming mouse. Marvin is a natural born artist, Fran thought, everyone else is just a kid at art school.

"They look amazing," Fran said.

"The Dorothy one is ridiculous!" he said. Fran wanted to lean against him. As he scratched his head, Fran could see a few exhilarating inches of his stomach and the hairs that grew there. She wouldn't have minded being one of those hairs. She would have been good as one of those hairs, she thought. She would have been silent and still, and moved in the wind, and gotten flattened in the shower, and caught in the waistband of his pants, and smoothed by the hand of a girl . . . Fran leaned toward him until her leggings touched his jeans. Inside the bowl, the mice clawed at each other's costumes. "Let's give them their freedom," Marvin said.

In the field by the canal, the baby mice scurried away in their costumes. "I bet the other mice will worship them," he said.

"They will radically change mouse culture," said Fran. With Marvin, she felt she was playing with the world in the right way.

"They'll be the first mouse celebrities," he said. "I hope it doesn't get to them."

He's childish, but in a sexy, home-schooled-by-wolves way, thought Fran. She felt destined to be alone with him in the night. She struggled to remember which bra and underwear she was wearing. On Ridge Street, they leaned in different directions. His mind seemed dazzlingly blank.

"Can I walk you home?" Fran asked Marvin. The words sounded outrageous to her. They dangled gaudily in the silence.

"Why?" Marvin asked, laughing.

"I don't know," Fran said, blushing. She had made the wrong moment. But she was wearing her good bra. Her hair looked good too; she could see it in the windows of parked cars. It didn't matter. All her looks and artistic talent, and other qualities people had liked—*your so dreamy*, someone had written in her high school yearbook—none of it mattered. The *your so dreamy* guy had probably completely forgotten about her. She tried a smile to conceal what was happening behind her face.

"Okay, bye!" Marvin said. Tears burned her eyes. She watched the back of him as he walked away. His cool, uncaring back.

. . .

Paulina walked dreamily toward the Furniture Studios. Sex with Tim continued to be one of the more disappointing experiences of her life, but chasing Tim was electrifying and occupied her like a job. She touched her hair and liked how it felt. She must have had more than a dozen hair clips keeping it up, but the clips were dark and blended in with her hair. She passed the student store and the slick, new Graphic Design Studios. She passed high school skaters and spiritless adults.

It was one of those glorious days when Paulina had charmed the registrar into dropping her incompletes, and she felt high above the system. She did little actual work, but the scholarship of a dead art historian kept her funded. In the corner of her eye, she saw Sadie and Allison coming out of the mail room. She had neglected them these last few weeks, but now was ready to embrace them.

"Hello, beauties!" Paulina cooed while mentally chastising their fashion choices. Allison was wearing a bag-like dress. *She should really use a leave-in conditioner.* Still, Paulina walked toward them with open arms. Sadie glared at Paulina.

"I didn't see you at my apparel show," Sadie said. "Were you in the back or something?"

"Sorry, doll, I got caught up," Paulina said. Something was different about Sadie. Her bangs were swept off her forehead. She was growing out her bangs! Paulina applauded the move.

"You should have seen her dress," Allison said. "You missed out."

They stood on the mail room steps, staring at a disappointing clothing sale on the sidewalk. Paulina studied Allison's vacant face, and remembered befriending her in Foundation Drawing. Back then, Allison dressed like a Depression-era newsboy and read *The Stranger* during breaks. Allison didn't speak, in class or out of class, and her roommate made jokes about it. Her classmates called her the Stranger, but Allison didn't seem to care. Paulina wanted to open up Allison like a dusty, locked chest and hear whatever oddities hid inside her.

Stoned in Paulina's dorm room, Allison told Paulina what she thought of everyone in their class, and how her favorite romance wasn't one of her own, but between Jasper Johns and Robert Rauschenberg. When Paulina expected her to smile, Allison's lips merely twitched. It was an accomplishment to make her laugh.

Allison painted abstract oil paintings. Anytime something figurative emerged from the mess, she blotted it out. She examined the paintings for hours, making sure none of her marks had mistakenly formed any conceivable face. They were chaotic paintings with jarring color choices. The paint was so thick in places it took years to dry. Paulina remembered dragging Sadie to Allison's studio sophomore year and watching Sadie tense up, afraid of getting paint on her clothes.

Back then, Allison thought Sadie a total flake, and Paulina did nothing to defend her.

"Were you with Fran?" asked Allison. A headache spread behind Paulina's eyes and there was a wild burn in her chest.

"This isn't about Fran," Paulina hissed. "It's about her stupid dresses."

"Why are they stupid? Because they have nothing to do with you?" Sadie's voice rose to a troubling pitch. Sadie was the first real friend Paulina had made at school. Many times they'd gotten dressed in Sadie's dorm and survived the walk to the goth club in heels.

"Keep it down," said Paulina. "You sound like a malfunctioning hair dryer." Freshmen hovered around the clothing sale. A girl tried on a long green sweatshirt and declared it her "soul outfit." A cloud of hatred exuded from Allison and Sadie, but Paulina pretended she couldn't feel it. "Fashion here bores me," Paulina said. "It's always a dress made out of recycled bottles and cans, or something 'inspired by nature.'" Telling them off was exhilarating. It felt like cutting the sickly branches off a magnificent tree.

"You're being cruel," Allison said, pulling her lifeless hair behind her ear, "as usual. First you ditch Julian and now us. Just admit you're in love with Fran!"

Allison never stood up to Paulina like this. It created bad lines in her forehead.

"Your new work looks like a sad child's finger painting," Paulina told Allison. "I just thought you should know."

"That means a lot, coming from a sad child!" Sadie screamed. The three had fought before, but never with this much contempt, and never in front of the mail room, where people had gathered to watch.

"I can't believe I wanted Eric to meet you," Sadie said.

"Eric?" Paulina asked. It felt beneath her to acknowledge him.

"God! I've only told you a million times!" Sadie said. "My boyfriend. He lives in Chicago. He's visiting this weekend."

Paulina sighed loudly.

"You don't even like yourself," Allison said, and they started walking away.

"I love myself!" Paulina shouted after them.

Her headache pounded on. It was an elite headache, she told herself. She'd have to shoo people away from it—it was all hers! People leaving the mail room stepped around her and she made no attempt to get out of their way. They can have each other, Paulina thought. I've got Fran.

Julian leaned against the brick wall of the Painting Building. Paint-stained cigarette butts were stuffed in a gap in the sidewalk. The weather was breezy and warm and made him feel he could will things into existence. The pretty boy walked out, the one Julian had wanted for his film, but had never asked.

Fran pushed open the heavy studio door.

"I've been waiting for you," Julian said breathlessly, unable to lie. All week he had walked in a daze, addicted to the idea of her. When he talked to Fran in his head, he spoke in a low, suggestive voice. He'd hung around the library waiting for her and never saw her.

"What? Shut up!" Fran said. She fleetingly wondered if he loved her, and decided he just wanted to sleep with her. Either way, it put her deeply at ease. She saw herself the way he saw her. This happened without her trying. She often felt the impression she gave off. Sometimes it was one of shyness and pretension, but through Julian's eyes she saw herself as independent and cool. She looked at him and he smiled. She started to walk down the street and he kept her stride. He asked her about her paintings and her semester and what freshman dorm she'd been in. She reminded him they'd taken the same art history class sophomore year.

"Are you hungry?" he asked as they passed the cafeteria.

"No." He was almost handsome. She was walking to her apartment. She hesitated. "Where are we going?"

"You tell me."

Fran rolled her eyes and allowed him to walk her home. They stood awkwardly at her door. Apollo crossed the street and they both stared at him. "One time at Riff's, I watched him play pinball for hours," Julian said.

"Was he good?"

"Phenomenal. I wanted to use him in a movie of mine, but he got totally paranoid about it when I asked," Julian said. Fran tried to imagine Julian at Riff's, Julian with Paulina, but couldn't.

"What was the film about?" Fran asked. She didn't listen to his lengthy answer. She watched her face in her dark bedroom window. It was furrowed in pretend concentration. The longer they stood there, the more it seemed she might let him in. Anxiety fidgeted through her body. She ran her finger along the jagged edge of her house key. When he wished her a good night, she was extremely relieved. She quickly unlocked her door and went inside.

From the peephole, she watched him smile. He was too tall to date. It was Marvin she loved. Things were building with Marvin. The mice + the gloves isn't something that just happens every day, she thought. If mice + gloves happens to people, they're meant to be together. Still, she was high off Julian's attention. She felt pretty without needing to see it in a mirror. She felt like she was great at painting, but had no desire to paint.

5

When Fran asked Paulina what it had been like with Julian, Paulina paused to remember. They were in the library looking at books of old paintings. "All the physical stuff was good," said Paulina.

"Yeah?"

"All the physical stuff was great." In that moment, Paulina wanted Julian, wanted to have him around. Julian was funny sometimes. Sometimes he'd made her laugh. He'd made her feel important. As if it were she who graced the dollar coin, instead of that Indian woman. She watched Fran twirl her hair, and resented how Fran's naïve questions kept dredging Julian back up. Paulina wanted to talk about *them*.

This semester, Fran's teacher was a boisterous woman painter who told them to "get weird and get wild." The woman's most famous work was a video of natural disasters edited to a soundtrack of awkward karaoke mistakes. In Fran's midsemester meeting, she told Fran she was straddling the edge of painting "good" and painting "bad," and urged Fran to choose a direction and not look back.

In the studio, James was playing the Beach Boys' *Smile* for the millionth time that week. Fran could hear someone relentlessly sanding a wooden panel. She painted Marvin from memory. It actually looked like him this time! But she got self-conscious her class would see, so covered his face with a beard, and made his eyes pink, covering each color with another color until the connection was lost.

She kept her face down as she painted, but could hear Marvin talking with someone (James?) across the room. "First you rip off its legs," it sounded like James said. She strained to hear them. "A boy's first stereo," Marvin said, or something like that. Fran took her brush to the brush-cleaner machine, just to get closer to their voices. She cleaned and cleaned her brush until they stopped talking.

"Hey," she said, leaning over Marvin's studio wall, where he was rubbing a chocolate bar over an immaculate white canvas.

"Hey," he said, but did not look up from his big scribbly lines.

Fran imagined a whole gallery of paintings like this. Critics would say, "Cy Twombly meets Willy Wonka!" Fancy people would buy the paintings and hang them in their dining rooms. People would hang the paintings over their beds and glance at them while they were having sex. The art school would buy one of the paintings to hang in their museum and a mouse would smell the chocolate. One of the famous costumed mice!

"Do you think the mice are still wearing their outfits?" she asked him.

"I bet the other mice have bit them off by now," he said matter-of-factly.

Fran ate ice cream at the cafeteria with Julian, anxious that people would see them. She hadn't memorized his face yet. Each time she looked at him he looked different from what she expected. Freshmen sat around in groups having the time of their lives. Some had never dyed their hair before, or worn their bikini top as a shirt. Julian looked at Fran, his eyes shining.

"I like someone else," Fran said.

"Impossible," Julian said.

"You probably don't know him," she said.

"Does he like you as much as I do?" Julian asked.

"No," Fran said laughing. "It's hard to tell. He's really spacey."

"Spacey, huh?" Julian leaned toward her as he spoke, and though so much of her rejected him, she wanted to let him love her. He seemed like he knew how. She looked down at her melted ice cream. She couldn't have Paulina if she had Julian. Paulina was the smartest, strangest person she'd ever met. Paulina talked about cavemen times as if she'd really been there.

Julian held Fran's hand. "What about Paulina?" she asked.

"I don't think about her anymore," Julian said.

"She's cool," Fran said. "I mean she's crazy, but I really get a kick out of her, you know?" Julian touched her chin. Again, Fran saw herself the way he saw her and it looked infinitely better than how she saw herself.

They walked into the quad, a courtyard covered in ceramic tiles and relief sculptures of naked women and moon faces. "Freshman year, I thought this was a Gaudian paradise," Fran said. Students were posing with cigarettes on dorm steps. Unsightly faux-leather portfolios leaned against the brick wall. Julian pulled Fran close to him. The air was thick with the freshmen's ideas and enthusiasm. "Are you going to kiss me?" she asked. She beamed at him and he kissed her. Her eyes took her to a regal, shaded place.

Paulina pressed her face to the window of the Furniture Studio, where Tim's rickety table was being critiqued. Tim nodded robotically in the corner. Paulina leaned against a streetlight, bored, thirsty, and missing Art History III. The sky was black and friendless. Paulina missed Allison and Sadie and punished them in her mind. She imagined herself the queen of Egypt and Allison and Sadie toiling in the sun, hauling bricks on their backs, begging for forgiveness.

Out of the darkness, the Venus Flytrap approached. Paulina had never seen her near a campus building. She was wearing striped pants and a huge poncho. Her wild hair hung in the air like a halo. "I know what you call me," the Venus Flytrap said. Paulina watched as Tim left through a side door with his friends. "And I like it, but I'm not too crazy about you."

There was an impenetrable misunderstanding between them. Paulina would never comprehend it. She wouldn't ask. She wanted to call out to Tim, but the Venus Flytrap paralyzed her. The girl looked at her expectantly. Tim was walking farther and farther away.

"Don't you talk?" the Venus Flytrap asked.

"Yeah," Paulina said, "all the time."

The Venus Flytrap scoffed. "Congratulations," she muttered.

Paulina hesitated.

"I can see right through you," the girl said. The girl was like a boardinghouse for misfit spirits. Paulina wasn't the only one who thought so. "Why did you come to art school if you don't make art?" the girl asked.

"For the memories," Paulina said. She'd meant it to seem

snappy, but it came out sentimental. Once she had seen the Venus Flytrap eat a live fish from Eileen's fish tank. Eileen had been upset about it, but what was there to do? It was at a party and everyone had loved it.

The girl laughed at her, then turned and left.

Paulina rushed to Tim's house thinking of things she could have said. She had modeled herself after the Venus Flytrap, but she hated her. What misuse of my time, she thought angrily. She had embarrassed herself. She had been weak like Fran. She had acted like a sophomore, not a junior. She had acted like a freshman deciding between graphic design and illustration, like someone who lived off a meal plan, who kept an online diary, someone with themed socks.

Tim opened the door a crack. "Yo, bad time," he said. Paulina could hear Cassie's voice inside.

"I walked all the way here," Paulina said, exasperated. "And I have a stone in my shoe. It feels like it's never a good time."

"Exactly. It's never a good time. I'm with Cassie, remember?" He sneered at her. She gave him the finger and he shut the door.

Paulina felt icy and dead. Cassie was a sculpture major. Sculpture majors think they're so far out, Paulina thought as she wandered down the street. Sculpture majors loved nothing more than taking up space. They clogged rooms with sloppy abstractions. They destroyed their computers. They damaged hallways dragging heavy plaster pieces to show friends. They had all kinds of filth under their fingernails.

The streets were deserted like a movie set. Paulina remembered how she and Julian had made the small town into a big joke. Each store seemed ridiculous—the store that sold tights and sunglasses, the fancy hotdog place. She and Julian had towered over the town. But lately she had forgotten all that. She'd just been living in it, taking it seriously.

Fran's apartment was totally dark. Paulina could see this from far off, but still walked up the steps and leaned against Fran's doorframe defeated. She rang the doorbell idly, just to touch something and make a sound. *Where was Fran? Drawing Marvin's likeness with a needle? Competing in the hair-twirling Olympics?* Paulina felt homeless. Glory was getting harder and harder to find. She scratched her name into the chipping paint on Fran's door.

Walking home, she saw Eileen drive by in Sadie's car but didn't wave. The world bored her. She wanted to be transformed. She needed sex, or drugs, or dancing—something that pushed the old self aside and made the new self gleam. She wanted to reclaim the red boots she'd given Sadie. The boots would torture her ankles but alleviate her mind. Paulina imagined Sadie with the other apparel majors, stressing/not eating. In her purse on her key ring, she felt for the cold key to Sadie's house.

Outside Sadie's window, Paulina saw Sadie and Allison eating pizza with a boy. He was handsome and wore a shirt that said TODAY IS A GOOD DAY in a faux handwritten font. Paulina was shocked to see the boy. It was how Sadie had said—he had green eyes and shaggy hair. The dining room was lit with candles. Paulina felt a sticky, static dread.

The boy squinted at Paulina through the window. She shrank back into a bush. She knew he wouldn't understand her, that his presence would evoke small talk and easy jokes. Sadie was wearing a preposterous SUPERTHRIFT costume that shouldn't have been revived. It clung to her like mermaid skin. She was pathetically in love with the creature in the T-shirt. They were holding hands under the table. Paulina watched them like a nature documentary.

Julian's apartment was one room plus a bathroom. In the corner, a mini fridge buzzed underneath a fake marble counter. On one wall hung a charcoal drawing of a school shooting. "Creepy!" Fran said.

Julian laughed. "Part of a series I did for my drawing class."

"How was the crit?" she asked.

"Awkward."

Fran couldn't tell if this pleased him or pained him. His bookcase was filled with sci-fi books and religious texts. A layer of dust coated everything but the bed. Fran couldn't imagine Paulina there.

Julian sat on his bed and pulled Fran to him. She noticed a picture of a Caravaggio painting that had been cut from a Caravaggio calendar and taped to the wall. She stared at a poster of a bearded man in a sweater.

"Who's that?" she asked.

"Alejandro Jodorowsky," he said.

"Who's he?"

"Crazy Chilean filmmaker."

She thought they would drink something or smoke something, but nothing was offered.

His body was pale. Any muscle he had was one needed to move. They kissed. He was almost handsome. He was handsome. Julian undressed her and her mind went limp. "You're so beautiful," he said. "You have amazing breasts." Sincerity felt queer at the school. Romance felt foreign. She ran her hand over his short dark hair. With her eyes closed, Julian was everyone, Paulina and Marvin, the world wanting Fran. This feeling colored her completely. Wanting proof, she stuck her hand in his boxers. Gripping his erection, she thought, *Mine*. She felt graceful behind her eyes. She was barely aware of what she was saying, but they did talk. They complimented and teased each other. His intense attention, his want to please her, it made her brave and powerful.

"I can't believe you are fucking that freak," Gretchen said. Fran's eyes danced from tree to tree. Her breasts felt amazing. "He's weird," Gretchen said.

"Good," Fran said as they walked into Utrecht. "No one will steal him away from me."

"In Drawing II, he only drew tragedies. Bad sign." Fran ignored her. "I'd rather get HIV from a dead warlock," Gretchen mumbled.

Fran laughed. "You sound just like Paulina!" she said.

Gretchen glared at Fran. Fran blushed.

"That's the only good part of this," Gretchen said, examining a set of expensive markers.

"What?"

"That you stole Julian from Paulina like she stole Andrew from me," Gretchen said with satisfaction.

"But she broke up with Julian."

"It doesn't matter. She's a sociopath."

"Well, don't tell anyone about me and him," Fran said. "Okay?"

"What do you care?"

"I'm sort of friends with her," Fran said, sweating.

"Finally, you admit it," Gretchen said. "I saw you guys dancing at a party once and wanted to throw up."

"What was I supposed to do? There was no one cool in Norway! I couldn't help it. We just hit it off."

"Hit it off? No one hits it off with her. It takes a lobotomy to be friends with her. Have you *seen* her friends?"

"I'm sorry," Fran said, but she wasn't. She felt Gretchen was the kind of girlfriend she would be offered again and again by the adult world, the real world, but Paulina was someone truly original, someone who existed only once.

"I'm over it," Gretchen said, trying out a black ink pen on the sample paper stuck to the shelf. She wrote her name in perfect cursive. "The important thing is you're dating Julian. It will ruin her life." She smiled.

Even after receiving Julian's affection, Fran remained fixated on Paulina. Paulina was like part ship captain, part call girl. Once Fran spent a whole party watching her, unable to name what was so impressive. Fran was terrified of Paulina finding out about Julian. Sometimes she would have dinner with Paulina, let Paulina walk her home, and then, when she was sure Paulina was out of sight, run to his house.

Fran lay on Julian's chest, asking him about Paulina.

"She fancied herself a wild lover," Julian said.

Fran giggled. "How?" she asked, stroking the coarse hairs under his arms.

"She was always thrashing about like there was a great passion within her, but somehow I doubted the passion."

Fran wanted to ask if there was a great passion in *her*, but it was a damning question. First, she would create a great passion. She was almost there. In bed with Julian, all her concerns flattened into a cracker.

"I'm going to tell her," Fran said. "You think it will go okay?"

"It could be awful, to tell you the truth. Like her in an awful mood, tromping about like a robot on the wrong setting."

"My Norwegian princess!" Paulina exclaimed when Fran found her in the library. "Look at this hairstyle!" Paulina said, pointing excitedly to a painting in a Velázquez book. "Isn't it amazing? I'm going to write my final on ancient hairdos." She grinned at Fran. "These girls are like hair gods!"

"How's it going with Tim?" Fran asked nervously.

Paulina sighed. "Honestly? It sucks." Paulina leaned dramatically against the bookcase behind her. "Sex with Julian was a million times better."

Fran's throat tightened. She'd expected Paulina to tire herself out praising Tim. Fran had grown used to hearing about Tim—his hands rough from sanding, how sawdust fell off his clothes like a kind of masculine powder.

"I gave up on Tim. He was completely unavailable to me. Anyway, what's happening with that, with Marvin?" Paulina asked.

"Nothing."

"That boy needs to get his dick checked at Health Services. Seriously! Who could resist you? Your silhouette should replace the school logo."

Fran opened her mouth to tell her, but Paulina was distracted, watching two girls covertly rip pages from a book. "I think Sadie and Allison have finally decided to ask for my forgiveness," Paulina said. "They asked me to come over. I had completely forgotten we weren't speaking." She turned suddenly, and looked into Fran's eyes. Fran stared back in terror. She had always been afraid of Paulina, even in Norway— afraid of her temper, her hasty dismissals, but also afraid of her affection. Once Paulina endorsed something, she raised it too high in her regard. Fran always felt exposed around her, that Paulina knew too well Fran's desires and insecurities.

"I should really go to studio."

Paulina made a face. "Promise me you'll come to Sadie's party tonight."

Fran found it impossible to say no.

6

"Allison saw them at Thai Dream," Sadie told Paulina. The three girls sat on lawn chairs on Sadie's porch. Below them, the students biked and walked to class.

"They're definitely together," Allison said with satisfaction.

"We thought you should know," said Sadie, beaming.

They hadn't apologized. Instead, when Paulina arrived, they'd hugged her stiffly, then told her of this poisonous development. Her face faltered. She forced a laugh. She pictured Fran naked and got the wind knocked out of her.

"Are you okay?" Allison asked.

"You look bad," noted Sadie. She remembered how Paulina looked when they'd first met, before Paulina had redone herself. Paulina's hair had been a ball of frizz. In the bathroom, she'd try to mat it down with water. She hadn't yet learned to carry her weight with power, and danced clumsily at Artist Ball. For a few weeks, she'd tried to get people to call her Lina, but no one would.

Paulina sunk into a primal, hateful area of her consciousness.

"What is it about my porch?" said Sadie. "When I'm up here I feel like I'm deciding who will get into heaven." They watched their classmates walk by in insignificant groups. Paulina sat frozen in her chair.

"It's actually really perfect. They're both corny and have no instinct for fashion," Paulina said. A muscle twitched in her face. Nils walked by, and normally Paulina would have shouted out to him, or at least criticized him to them, but she was silent. "She's ruined everything," Paulina said.

"Maybe she'll die," Allison said lightheartedly.

"She'd haunt me. Though she's no great mind, she'd figure out how."

"What if *you* died?" Sadie asked. Paulina gave her a nasty look. "No, I mean like, then *you* could haunt *her*."

That Fran could find happiness with Julian was excruciating to Paulina. Fran was adding on to a project Paulina had halted. Hadn't she mined all there was? She took her blanket out from her bra.

"You still have that bit of rag?" Sadie asked, pitying her.

"It looks like Joseph Beuys's wolf blanket," Allison said, "but smaller."

"This blanket was given to me by a spirit in the night," Paulina said. A smile fleetingly premiered across her face before drooping like a dead plant. Allison rolled her eyes.

"Let's go," Sadie said. Already they were tired of her again.

"Fine, go. But I feel poisoned and might do something horrid we'd all regret."

"Like what?" Allison asked. Paulina wanted more of a reaction. She sat silently, depriving them of her answer.

"Then come to the cafeteria with us," Sadie said impatiently.

Paulina refused. "It's always crawling with freshmen in their high school wardrobes."

"If you want to hang out before the party, we'll be at Eileen's. You know the address."

"No, I don't. I forgot it," Paulina said unhappily.

"You know it!" Sadie said, gathering her things. "Listen, stay here all you want, but lock up when you go." Paulina gave them a pained look, but still they left her.

She sat on the porch for a miserable half hour, the plastic bands of the lawn chair sticking to her thighs. The dread she'd felt in little packets over the last few months now traveled to her from a greater source, in huge waves from the town's reservoir of dread, sending dread meant for other people, a collective dread her body absorbed with no immunity. She pictured the dread like smoke or oil. Oil that turned into smoke. She felt like a ruin of a woman, like a cold, empty cave. She tried to draw up a life plan, but a mean magnet sat on her brain, preventing her from thinking forward. She was stuck in the ugly cell of the moment.

Eventually, Paulina rose from the chair, stormed into the room Sadie used as her closet, and ransacked the shoe rack for the red leather boots.

In a daze, Paulina marched downtown. Naïve bitch, Paulina thought, and pictured Fran laughing in Norway. Fran dancing at the Color Club. Too easily, she imagined Fran naked. Gather your thoughts, bitch, Paulina thought. *I love myself I love myself I love myself,* Paulina chanted to herself. *Do the breath thing, get your breath straight.* She tried to remember what it was that she usually summoned to keep her from crying, but instead pictured the Holocaust—the thing she pictured to stop laughing during a lecture. She made a sound between laughing and crying. Two flat-chested girls turned to stare.

She was surprised to find she knew his schedule and in what classroom he was watching mediocre films. She burst in the door and they all looked up, squinting like shrews at the light. He was slumped in the back row. Paulina marveled at the weird creatures who had chosen film/animation/video as their major. Beastly looking people she recognized from

freshman year hadn't transferred as she'd assumed; they'd actually been holed up here, tinkering with buttons.

Paulina saw that none of them knew how to use makeup,
that the boys were clinging to their eccentricities, that the girls
were clutching their insecurities dear. They wore big T-shirts
and had stringy hair. Two of them wore chain wallets. There
were a few girls and guys who had good posture and clever
eyes, but they stood out like swords in a room of noodles.
Someone in the front row reached out to touch Paulina's dress
and she swatted the creature's hand. The girl whimpered and
sat back in her seat. "Brains!" Paulina managed, and an unre-
markable middle-aged man looked amusedly to Julian.

With big steps he walked around his sleepy, unwashed
classmates and met Paulina in the hall.

"Fuck me," she said, "in a video-editing room, my place,
your place." She swayed aggressively.

He recognized the embroidered silk undershirt she wore
over a faded sundress. Her lips were scrunched tightly together. Her body seemed braced to engulf him. "No," he said.
Her heart beat violently in her chest. She waited for him to say
more, but he held himself still. He could hear the audio from
his classmate's film.

The dread was lodged in her throat. The oil turned to
smoke. "Take your life," she said shaking, "and have it *far*
away from me." Straightening to a height he'd never seen, she

stomped her boots down the hall, each step making a terrible crack.

At Sadie's party, the kitchen floor was covered with mud from everyone's shoes. The wallpaper and curtains clashed in discord. Paulina was in a circle of acquaintances. "I can't get excited about small dogs," she said to the group. She'd changed into one of her more preposterous costumes—her Guatemalan war dress, Sadie called it. Bright knit fabric frayed over her cleavage where she'd cut the dress with scissors. Her hairdo relied on all her hair clips to create a "velvet rope" effect—again, Sadie's words.

After leaving Julian, Paulina had picked up a random boy outside the Film Building who wore his T-shirt tucked in his jeans. The boy had a number of nervous tics, and looked like he animated dragons all day. During the short walk to his place, he'd talked good-naturedly about his classes as if he were giving a school tour. When they were finally in his small bedroom, he gave Paulina an impish, Fran-like shrug. She pushed him onto his made bed. He seemed grateful for her direction. It felt to Paulina that she was giving the boy's narrow bed something it had always wanted but never thought it would have. For a few minutes it made Paulina feel better—the boy acted like he had undergone a religious conversion—but soon Paulina's good feeling crashed and she felt quite doomed again.

Fran arrived at Sadie's party dressed for spring, and skipped over to Paulina, who evaded her hug and pushed her into the wall. "You bore me," Paulina said, and the crowd around them backed up.

"Paulina," Fran said blushing, but Paulina turned swiftly on her heels, and as if attached to her with string, the group followed her into the dancing room. Even from the next room, Fran could hear her theatrics.

"The stars in our sky are far, far inferior to the stars of our ancestors," Paulina said and laughed. Every time Fran looked over, Paulina glared back. Fran drank beers and the beers made her tilt.

Marvin wandered through the door. Fran walked shakily over to him, believing he was the Savior. When she reached him, she realized he was just an undiscovered model with a creative mind. Still, his smile unwound the knots in her.

"This party sucks," Fran said. "Everyone is just making up theories."

"I'm no fan of theories," said Marvin. He looked with deep interest at the mud pattern on the linoleum. Sadie burst by, stupidly drunk, covered in jewelry. "He said he loves me!" she cried, carrying a splayed-open laptop into the next room. Fran's glassy eyes were fixed on the wall. *But she dropped Julian so casually! She spent so much time complaining about him. She hadn't seemed at all attached.*

"You okay?" Marvin asked.

"This party just sucks," Fran said, avoiding his gaze, "but I have to stay," she said. "I have to talk to someone," she said, "about something sort of stupid," she said. She wanted to latch on to him. He looked at her blankly.

Paulina sat like a princess on the ottoman. Apollo walked by and Eileen ran after him, holding a bag of cocaine. Fran felt disoriented. Girls from her studio eyed her with curiosity. Fran had no idea if her hair looked good. She touched it and couldn't tell. She searched for a reflective surface.

One night in Norway, after Paulina had styled Fran's hair, they had shown each other their breasts and complimented them. Fran had felt they had always known each other and always would. Now Fran walked up to Paulina and everyone cleared away except Allison, who sat unmoving. In the kitchen, girls took pictures of Marvin. "That's no way to treat beauty," Paulina said and Fran silently agreed.

"I know you hate me right now," Fran said.

"Don't flatter yourself," said Paulina, playing with a bracelet on her wrist that made a sound like rain.

"I didn't think you liked him anymore, but I should have asked."

"Who?" There was a pause in which neither moved. Paulina fixed her eyes on her bracelet, shoplifted from Nordstrom. Of course she *liked* him. She loved him, loved both of them, but this thought snapped back into the dark unknowing place of her. Bits of conversation made her turn to the other room where Eileen was humping the floor "breakdancing." Someone was saying, "It's that gluey stuff you spread onto the solder and the metal so they bond." A girl said, "I found a cockroach in their toilet and saved it with a piece of toilet paper." "I was an absolute animal in LA!" Apollo yelled and beat his fist in the air.

Paulina turned back to Fran. "I *don't* like him. He's boring. His life is useless. His apartment sucks," Paulina said, looking at her fingernails. Fran rolled her eyes. "I mean he's nice. I think he's nice. Do you think he's nice?" Paulina asked Allison, who was slowly packing weed into a bowl. Each time she said nice, it sounded like a boring, stupid thing to be. Allison smirked.

Sadie plopped down next to Paulina. "The best night of my life!" Sadie said, and threw her head on Paulina's lap. Paulina mindlessly stroked Sadie's long black hair.

"He loves me, Fran!" Sadie said happily.

"I'm really sorry," Fran said, her eyes filling with tears.

"Enough," Paulina said waving her away. "You're ruining the party."

Paulina's hate balled like a fist, willing Fran to leave, but Fran still stood before her. Paulina glared holes in Fran, watching her tears drip. Finally Fran turned and left. Allison blew out smoke. "She is actually pretty ordinary," Paulina told Allison. "She deceived me by dressing so eccentrically. A lisp doesn't make you charismatic."

Dean and Troy arrived, rescuing the party from its familiarity. In the dark, they were all renewed. They sweated through their outfits. They sniffed a bottle of shoe polish that gave a staggering two-minute high. People made out in the corners of Sadie's apartment. Apollo put his arm around Paulina's waist, and she draped herself over his twitchy shoulders. She touched his shaved head and it felt eelish and undid her.

She imagined sex with him while he pitched a book he was writing about the government. "Nineteen fifty-five, they dropped three hundred thousand fever mosquitos from a plane over Georgia. Then they made a bomb made of fleas. It burst open on the plane. Those are facts. But what is their aim? How are they going to control the world with bugs? The facts are out there, they just need to be interpreted." The novelty of Apollo was evaporating. "Where's Sadie?" Paulina asked Allison.

"Phone," Allison said. She lay on Sadie's couch looking at her hands. The party's excitement had expired, but while most people gathered their things, believers tried to revive the party by flinging themselves around the room and sniffing shoe polish.

Eileen motioned Paulina into the kitchen, but Paulina turned and left. Apollo followed her onto the street. Outside it smelled like skunk. He kissed her and she let him. His tongue jabbed around her mouth. She had a vision of a charcoal drawing she'd done of him freshman year: he was crouched on a box, his uncircumcised penis in shadow. Paulina burst out laughing.

"What?" Apollo asked.

"It stinks out here."

"I'm taking you to my hideout," said Apollo. Paulina wanted to ridicule him, but she also wanted him.

"You'll have to wear a blindfold, though," he said.

"I wouldn't have it any other way," she said.

"No one knows where I crash." He took his American flag bandanna out of his pocket.

At first, Paulina kept track of the direction they walked, but now she no longer cared. She hadn't really liked Fran as an equal she told herself. She had just been entertained by Fran's youngness. She remembered Julian as a time suck. What had they even talked about? Lazing on the couch, saying nothing, nothing interesting. She remembered how she had lorded over Smith and laughed out loud.

"What?" Apollo asked.

"Nothing," she said.

He held her still. She heard his keys. A door creaked open. Inside, it smelled familiar. "Okay, up these stairs, go slow." She managed up the steps. *Lovers pass over quickly. Yes, there is a turnover rate for lovers.* As proof, she strained to remember her first boyfriend from junior high and could not, but then with a flash—*Aldon Landry*—she remembered his green backpack, Alice in Chains tattoo, and all that went with it.

Paulina lay on an air mattress in Apollo's cramped attic space. Now that they were done and talking, his body seemed smaller to her. He rocked from side to side. He couldn't lie still. "All of you are just freaky rich kids with drawing talent, but no one cares about that kind of talent anymore. The queen does not need her portrait done, thank you very much." He laughed.

"Why rich?" Paulina asked.

"Someone has sent you off to draw portraits! Someone has tricked you into thinking it's a life plan." Paulina's eyes fixed on the roof beams and she realized they were in the attic of the College Building.

"Don't you all know about cameras? A camera does the same thing you guys are doing."

"I know. I completely agree," she said. She felt she was the only student in the school who knew art was unnecessary.

"Art is an adolescent impulse to busy oneself with oneself," she said. His eyes stared off. "How many other portrait painters have you slept with?" she asked.

"You think you're the only one?" He laughed exaggeratedly. "Hell no! When I'm up there, I'm advertising my whole deal. How old am I?" He turned to her, grinning. "How old do I look?" He propped himself up on his elbow and started isolating and flexing his muscles. She looked away to the roof beams. *The College Building or the Foundation Building.* He'd decorated the space with flags and discount sheets. Unopened instant soups surrounded his rice cooker. There was something congealed in a pan. "What is that?" Paulina asked.

"Whaddya think it is?" he asked. She cringed. He laughed in her ear. Library books were piled by the side of his air mattress. A cow skull sat on his dresser.

"Did you steal that from the Nature Lab?" she asked.

"You think animals only exist in the Nature Lab? You think there are more alive things than dead things? Guess again," he said. She laughed. "Guess again."

Paulina thought too much about Fran. She crumbled like a salt woman, making her computer show her revolting things, then asking it honest, naïve questions about her body and the Middle East conflict. At SUPERTHRIFT, she searched for something revolutionary and left wearing the gaudy jacket of a drum major.

Twice Paulina saw Fran with Julian. The first time they were kissing on someone's doorstep. Paulina averted her eyes immediately, like she'd seen a headless person on the highway. The second time, she arrived early to a movie and saw them, still in the theater after the credits. She didn't stay for the movie. She rushed home thinking, I will become a myth who murders old loves. At home, she stripped off her clothes and put on her red boots. She imagined setting the theater on fire. It is vain of me, she thought, angrily snapping spaghetti in half.

She recalled, at first in bits, and then in an overwhelming wave, fond memories of Julian. She remembered how stoic he was and how she overturned him. How they insulted their classmates in private and exchanged knowing looks in public. She remembered a time when she'd sat for Julian and when he was done drawing, instead of critiquing it to him, she just complimented him. How exciting it must have been for him to lose his virginity to someone who knew what she was doing and didn't care about getting dirty or making noise.

Afraid of running into Fran at the college library, Paulina started going to a small library far from campus, in an area messy with construction. The library was cold and sleek. Paulina sank between two rows of books. She stretched her legs.

She remembered Fran dancing in front of the jagged mirror and smashed an ant with her sandal. She applied makeup with a small foam cube. She said, "Fuck me, Julian," and, with her legs spread on the toilet, orgasmed quietly in the library bathroom stall.

7

In May, the Color Club boys graduated. There were extravagant parties every night. Parties where the Venus Flytrap set her final project on fire and Zane danced nude with underwear painted onto his body. Sadie and Allison gave the boys flowers. And then they were gone. One could walk the streets incessantly and never run into them. A family moved into the Color Club and started repairing and removing every wonderful thing about it.

The school's little society split and scattered for the summer. Fran heard that Paulina and Allison went to New York together, but she didn't know what they did there or where Sadie had gone. Julian TA'd film classes. The campus filled with high schoolers. Fran took a job at SUPERTHRIFT, stapling colored tags on to the clothing. Monday, green tags were half off. Tuesday it was blue tags. Fran and a high school girl drove the SUPERTHRIFT van to all the metal donation bins. Sometimes there was trash thrown in with the clothes—plastic bags of dog poop, dead plants, shattered picture frames.

Fran sublet her apartment to a grad student for the summer, and moved her things into Julian's. They spent every night together in an easy love. Fran didn't tire of watching him. His long legs, his short hair. She studied him. He wasn't a Greek god or oracle, or whatever Marvin was, but he was real, and smart, and completely hers. Every story he told her, she saved it in her mind as if she were going to write his biography, or tell it to their kids.

They tried to cook things for each other. They did their laundry in the same machines. They got so good at getting each other off that they could do it blindfolded or standing up, or quickly in an alley, or awkwardly on a big rock near the canal.

They neglected their art. They never worked. It was too hot on the weekends. They talked a lot about work. They imagined doing work with such concentration, as if work was done only in the studio of the mind. They lay in Julian's humid apartment, naked and dreaming.

"It won't be easy to get the money for my first film, but it will happen," Julian told Fran. "I'll be patient and stick with it. I'll do some shorts and get them into festivals. I won't use video. I'll intern for the masters."

Fran turned onto her back. The fan oscillated toward them

and away from them, blessing them and scorning them. "I'm going to get a nice studio with big windows. But first I might have to paint in my room or wherever I can. I'll get an apartment with a porch."

"Good. You should," he said.

"This year I'm going to be super focused and do really good work for my show." She could see herself doing work. She pictured herself blowing a stray curl out of her face, painting in nice dresses and ruining the dresses and not caring. She pictured the paintings she wanted to make and the things people would say about them. And how she would look next to the paintings, having made them. Carrying them around. She imagined living in Brooklyn or Portland with Julian, being grown-ups and hosting dinner parties and raising a puppy together. She imagined a wedding where everyone acted crazy and there were no adults. She imagined raising children in the woods, living off the grid, whatever that meant. Having a secret woods mansion. But running it off green energy.

"I'm never going to use violence for violence's sake or sex for sex's sake, but there is going to be sex and violence in these movies." Julian got up and went to the sink to get water. When he got back into bed, Fran wrapped herself around him.

"What if we moved to Canada after we graduate?" she said. "Wouldn't that be cool?" There were probably tons of trees in Canada. It was always so green on the map.

"I guess," he said. "Who knows."

Fran pouted. She went to the bathroom to look at her hair and it looked good. Her breasts were swollen because she was expecting her period, and they also looked good. She was interesting. People told her she looked like she was in a band. There was no reason he shouldn't want to live with her, and marry her and everything.

They saw each other so much that summer that the boredom became normal. They talked through the boredom. They criticized each other in their minds, and then a joke broke through the glass or a kiss did the unraveling work of a kiss. Sometimes they knew there was something better out there, sometimes they had the imagination to picture it, but they were lazy and liked each other. Finally they were part of a pair—someone would listen to whatever they said.

"Sampson is recommending me for this big Whitney residency award thing. All I need to do is fill out this application."

"Fill it out!" Julian nuzzled into her neck. Fran knew he thought she was unmotivated. He'd said so a few times. The application wasn't that complicated, but there were essay questions. No one had taught her how to write essays. It stressed her out. She felt absently for his dick and his balls. She ran her hand softly against his pubic hair, then on his thin thighs and bony knees.

"You know," he said, "I know something about you that I never told you."

"What?" she asked. She wanted to ask him to do the dishes. He hadn't done a dish in so long.

"I know about Blood Axe."

Fran laughed. It didn't make any sense. "What about Blood Axe?" she asked.

Julian danced his fingers up and down her back. "Everything about it," he said slyly. "The cabin, and Paulina, and the zebra-skin rug. How you lost your virginity to him and made Paulina keep it a secret." Fran wanted to die laughing. She pressed her face into his stomach. "Don't be embarrassed. I think it's super sexy. It was my first fantasy of you." Fran was incredulous. "I mean, I know his real name wasn't really Blood Axe. Blood Axe is some ancient Norwegian warrior. I looked it up. But that's what she called him, so that's how I thought of him."

Fran smiled in disbelief.

Julian elbowed her. "When were you going to tell me? I've been waiting for you to tell me," he said.

"But you've already heard the whole story," said Fran.

"I want to hear you tell it," he said. "Look how hard it gets me," he said.

She played with his erection, remembering her first time having sex in high school, and then called back the Blood Axe fantasy. All she could see were abs and hair. He'd had powers, too—she remembered. He'd been a time traveler, or something.

"It was a good way to lose it," she said. "He was very kind. The whole thing was dreamy."

"Dreamy like how?" he asked. "Were you drunk?"

"No, but I was seeing everything in this heightened way. When I met him, I could have just, like, taken a picture of him and moved on, but I could tell there was something mysterious and wonderful about him, so I lingered." She looked at him, gauging whether he bought the whole thing, and was charmed that he did. He kissed her and she kissed back.

"And after you, he had sex with Paulina?" he asked.

She nodded. "And after Paulina, Milo."

"No!" he said. She laughed.

"Yeah. Paulina didn't tell you that? Milo had never even kissed someone before. It really changed his work when he got back. He switched to sculpture." Julian shifted his weight. His eyes were filled with doubt. He started to object but Fran interrupted.

"She's something, right?"

"Who?" Julian asked.

"Paulina. She's like Cleopatra, but more squat."

"She's more like Humphrey Bogart."

"No!" Fran shook her head.

"I mean her voice is," said Julian.

"Yeah, her voice."

Senior year started with no great event. After Paulina's summer in New York, the college town seemed even more pitiful. Sadie and Allison took pictures of it to remember, but Paulina wanted to watch it shrink in the rearview mirror of a vehicle speeding away. She started hanging out in the dilapidated mill buildings downtown, where art dudes squeezed puff paint on flawed iron-casting projects and built couches and lived their dreams out in high ceilings and local fame, thrashing on drum sets, blowing their amps, going by names like Dog Claw and Mystic. In these warehouses, there was often a Lego wall, a makeshift bathroom, and a desire for the world to end.

Mystic had graduated years before, but he stayed in town, playing noise shows and dating girls from the school. Paulina wasn't very attached to him, but she needed someone's dumb eyes on her when she lay in bed. Even in New York she'd thought daily about Julian and Fran. Mystic's loft bed had a ladder and a slide, and like other girls before her, Paulina usually took the slide. The bathroom had an exposed light bulb and a door with no lock. Instead of a toilet seat, there was a piece of wood with a hole cut in it. Beyond that was a series of rooms crammed with rotting packing materials.

Paulina slept at Mystic's most nights, avoiding campus when she didn't have class. She found it easy to ignore Fran, even early in the semester when Fran was still fool enough to wave at her in public. Paulina glided by her, thinking, *You trimmed my toenails in a past life* or *You will trim my toenails in the next life*. She saluted Julian when she saw him, as if they had served together in a war and she would always have his back.

She did well in her art history classes. She scared the sophomores in her printmaking class. She wasted hours with Sadie and Allison, styling their hair and listening to the trials and triumphs of their lives. When they left town for winter break, Paulina was especially bored. She recorded her orgasms on her computer and played them back for her amusement.

At the start of spring semester, Mystic's warehouse hosted a party. Paulina wore a sample dress Sadie had made that had one long sleeve and one short sleeve. Mystic's roommates decorated the main room with Christmas lights and big foam sculptures. Gradually the room filled with Paulina's classmates. Sadie and Allison arrived and huddled around Paulina while she talked shit about Mystic and his roommates. "They violated a cat yesterday. It was vile. I had to leave."

"Violated?" Sadie asked.

"They think they're rock stars, but they're abandoned children in a never-ending sleepover."

Despite everything, it still excited Sadie to be around Paulina. Things were revealed around her. People performed. Her curls seemed to contain the natural delight of the universe.

"Your hair looks awesome," Sadie said.

"Thanks! It's this new conditioner I—"

They all turned as Fran walked into the party. She was

wearing the jumper from SUPERTHRIFT. "Oh my God," Sadie said, "I love her outfit."

Paulina shook her head in disbelief. Fran looked stunning, like exceptional things would happen to her.

"Isn't that, like, a child's clothing thing?" Paulina said.

"I don't know what it is, but she can pull it off," Sadie said. Paulina wished she had ripped the jumper to shreds when she'd had the chance. She met Fran's eyes and both of them looked quickly away.

The dance floor was barbaric and free. Mystic shined a flashlight over the dancers. Paulina closed her eyes and replayed the compliments she'd received about her hair. She opened her eyes and saw Sadie dancing with Fran. Sadie's hand caressed Fran's curls and they danced, flitting around each other like preteens. Paulina raged inside herself. Why couldn't people stay where she put them? They were always pairing up to destroy her!

"Babe, meet Darlene," Mystic said. "She's an art history major too." Paulina glanced at the slight redhead before her. She had the figure of a pencil.

"Art history is dead," Paulina said and stormed off to find drugs.

Eileen and Paulina smoked weed in Mystic's room. A huge Gorgeous Cyclops poster covered a broken window. "Have you ever heard them?" Paulina asked Eileen. She didn't wait for an answer. "They are the absolute worst band I've ever heard. It's like they're allergic to melody. They played here for hours last weekend and then they stayed for days and days. They ate all my food."

Eileen passed the glass piece to Paulina. "Smoking weed makes me feel like an alien," she said. "Heroin makes me feel like I invented all of this myself."

Paulina examined her. "What are you, like painting or fashion or what?" Eileen answered, but Paulina was thinking about Fran. Why was Fran imprinted over all her thoughts? It was her face. And that lightness. Fran wasn't attached to the ground—a wind carried her. No. Fran was just a lonely child the woods had taken pity on. Paulina could picture Fran in the woods in Norway offering Paulina a hit off a glass piece.

Eileen's mouth was moving. Eileen was laughing. Eileen was wearing the same spandex jumpsuit she'd been wearing last time Paulina saw her. Paulina had a fantasy of her and Eileen taking over the party with force. Burning the bad parts of the warehouse. Falling in love with themselves. "Let's dance," Paulina said, pulling Eileen out of the room.

Marvin, Nils, and a bunch of people passed, but Paulina didn't bother saying hello. The dance floor was full of freshmen girls in flashy clothes. It didn't make sense. How did they already know how to dress? Paulina gawked at their bodies. They were shameless. How had they heard there was a party? How had they found the warehouse? One had a face tattoo. I bet Face Tattoo does heroin, Paulina thought. Paulina had often longed and failed to do heroin. She danced with little spirit.

Eileen mixed easily with the freshmen. Traitor, Paulina thought. She imagined Eileen doing heroin with Face Tattoo in a room with Oriental rugs and old records. She wondered where Tim was. If he'd ever gotten the picture she e-mailed him over the summer. If he had jerked off to it or deleted it. She imagined Tim in an orgy with the freshmen. Paulina had often longed and failed to be part of an orgy. Once at Smith something had started, but the RA had put a stop to it. Paulina's arms hung by her side. She watched Fran writhe around in the middle of the floor. Paulina wanted to break into the center with Eileen or Sadie or Face Tattoo and get everyone's attention.

Surrounded by people ecstatically dancing to Prince, Fran made out with Marvin. Paulina stared at them and felt feverish. She clutched the person next to her, a small girl in a tank top. The girl shook her off. The kiss kept going. Marvin's hands held Fran's hair. Her body was pressed against his. Arms and legs blocked Paulina's view, but every moment she could see some of the kiss.

8

Julian answered his door wrapped in his quilt. "She's making out with Marvin," Paulina said, her eyes flashing with life. His face fell. "At the warehouse party." She waited impatiently for his sadness to turn to lust.

Julian's chest was tight. His legs felt hollow. He wanted to close the door on her. Gossip was distasteful to him, and in the middle of the night it seemed petty and hysterical. "Who's Marvin?"

"You don't know?" Paulina scoffed.

Fran kissing another boy made no sense to Julian, but what could be expected from either girl? Both snuck off to house parties while he slept.

Paulina pushed past him. She surveyed the room and stood glaring at a new painting—one of Fran's half-assed attempts. From the beginning, Paulina had been unimpressed with Fran's paintings. Paulina could see them in the future, hanging crooked in lame coffee shops. She saw them ending up in trash bins outside Chinese restaurants. Garbage men would hold them up to each other and laugh.

Paulina couldn't decide if she should seduce Julian then and there or save it for when he looked less pathetic. Fran's presence permeated the room.

"Why are you here?" he asked, leaning against the doorframe.

"I fuck myself in honor of you," Paulina said.

He shifted his weight. He did not smile. She was wearing those stupid boots again. There was a big tear in her pantyhose, one he bet she'd made on purpose. He could see the shape of her breasts underneath the asymmetrical dress. Still, he could just go back to sleep. He let his quilt drag on the floor. He looked past her defiant sneer to the curls that surrounded it.

"Your hair," he said. "Your hair looks . . ." She knelt before him and felt a rush.

Skipping home after the party, Fran felt an insane feminine power. She imagined herself trying on outfits, and her body making the outfits better. In her own narrow bed, she daydreamed her kiss without Julian's snoring. Even during the kiss, she'd been daydreaming the kiss. The night had felt like a cool, dark holiday—as if by kissing Marvin she was saying yes to the night. But this would sound weak to Julian, sounded weak to her right now.

In the morning, Fran walked to Julian's. She crawled over to where he sat slumped on his couch. "Your place was too far from the party," she said.

He said nothing. It was obvious to him that she'd slept over at that guy's house. When she kissed him, his mouth closed. When she took her shirt off, he looked away. "Marvin," he said, pulling himself off the couch. Fran's heart beat unevenly.

"I know," she said. "I shouldn't have, but we were dancing." She drew this last word out, making her sound even more foolish to him. Girls at the school felt dancing was important and spiritual. He found it a pretentious flirtation.

Suddenly she seemed irrelevant in the greater course of his life. A blathering party girl. He wanted someone important. Someone who could see the world beyond. Someone who could name five countries in South America, or at least four. Someone capable of survival in any situation. Someone with endurance. He saw Fran floating through the rest of her life on a combination of luck and good genes. If she were a boy, if he weren't sleeping with her, would he even want her around? She was bland compared with Paulina. Sure, she was sweet, but that would wear off—had already worn off. He loved her, but maybe that said more about him than her. He was probably just good at loving. He felt intense fondness for her. Maybe it wasn't even love.

Fran held a certain unnamable trait, and it had inspired a whole love affair, and no, he couldn't exactly name it now, not precisely, but he knew the roots of it, the aspects that combined to make her attractive and intriguing, and this mixture wasn't made out of the big, extraordinary things, it just dabbled in those. It was her lisp, paired with the weird shit she said going to sleep, a smell he hadn't smelled on anyone before, but would probably smell on countless other girls, once he left the cramped college town.

"Kiss me," Fran pleaded.

"I no longer desire you," he said. She looked at him hopelessly. He squeezed her arm for a second, then dropped it. It fell to her side. She cried and he did nothing. He'd spent the morning crying and it no longer represented anything to him.

"I'm sorry!" she said. "I'm stupid!"

"I'm late," he said, waiting for her to leave.

"I love you," she said. He groaned and left for class, closing her in his apartment.

She waited for him to come back. When he didn't, she stuffed her face in his pillow, sobbing. When she grew bored of this, she sat in his desk chair twirling, examining his room, which felt entirely different from the night before. All his objects had turned against her—his sunken-eyed Buddha, his plastic laundry bin. The room barely tolerated her.

Fran saw something on the rug and her whole body felt hot. Without getting very close, she could see it was Paulina's student card. Fran picked it up. Paulina looked distracted in the picture. Her pale skin looked masklike. Red-eye gave her an eerie look. Paulina's lips were pursed as if about to speak. Fran felt an unbearable ache, as if the dead were pulling her heart. She slid the card in her wallet, beneath her own student card. They had been *dancing,* she thought again, but Julian did not understand dancing.

Paulina rejoiced when she saw Fran enter the town library crying. It was an old, decrepit library, too, where homeless people pretended to read and perverts sniffed books. Paulina walked to Julian's with a light heart. Big gray clouds crawled across the sky. She was supposed to work on her thesis paper, "Hairstyles through Art History." She wore the crazy drum major jacket.

Her confidence sagged when no one answered Julian's door. Paulina leaned against the scratchy siding of the house. She smoothed her eyebrows. She crouched as if to sit, but didn't want to dirty her Guatemalan war dress. She told herself she could work on her paper in her mind. She forgot the dirt and sat down, absently adjusting her bra, thinking about the hair history paper, how it was progressing. That Rousseau painting *War* had some funny hair, the one with the girl riding a horse.

She'd slept with Julian only a few times since he left Fran, but each felt like a victory. It was different with him now. It was always at his place and she didn't sleep over. She left in the night feeling like a witch who had created night. The kissing had changed too. They didn't kiss hello or good-bye. There were only the long wild kisses during sex, the experimental kisses that initiated sex, and the brain-dead kissing after sex. Paulina peered into Julian's first-floor neighbors' apartment. These neighbors were adults with actual careers. They'd put time and money into arranging a stylish living room, which sat in the dark like an abandoned hotel lobby.

The leaves on the trees rustled in that scared-horse, about-to-rain way. Julian was probably working on his senior film, Paulina thought, remembering him talking about it while she'd lain beside him, bored out of her mind. During this part of the semester, the film kids obediently held microphones and lights for each other, straining under the weight, convinced they were witnessing the authentic film magic they'd been chasing, and would chase into various disappointing careers. Meanwhile the director yelled and sighed and tried to manipulate his classmates into convincing performances, but it was like squeezing water from a stone, or so Julian said.

Paulina was standing up to leave when she saw Fran approaching. Her clothes looked slept in. Fran glared at Paulina's garish coat.

"Did you lose your troop?" Fran asked.

"When was the last time you showered? Your baptism?" Paulina asked.

Fran looked wearily into Paulina's bright eyes. She missed Julian's love. She craved the zen-ness of being rammed. The one time she'd seen Marvin, he'd waved noncommittally, like a classmate. In her studio, she'd started a painting of Paulina and turned her into a demon.

"Do you ever even fall in love?" Fran asked Paulina. "Or do you just live to conquer people's bodies?"

"The latter," Paulina said and laughed.

"You never even loved him, though! I love him," Fran said.

"What do you know of love? You are remote. Wind chimes drive you deep in reverie."

"Julian was my sexual awakening," Fran said.

"No shit!" Paulina said. "Who do you think taught him all that? Before he met me, he couldn't get a snowball wet." Paulina snickered. Fran blushed. She tasted blood in her mouth.

"He said the weight of you nearly crushed his ribs," Fran said. "He said you were always overacting."

A rush of embarrassment stunned Paulina. "I was only friends with you as a novelty!" she yelled. "How a child picks an ant from a pile of ants and makes it their pet for the afternoon."

"To be your friend is to be owned by you," Fran said, shaking.

"You're so pathetic. You will never be an artist. Success

will elude you! Everyone will forget you," Paulina said, putting a curse on her. "You will live nowhere! You will do nothing!" Fran cried into her arm and Paulina laughed like the demon in the painting.

Fran's face was red with tears, but she grew prettier through the crying. Beauty is given to the idiots, thought Paulina, and recalled watching Marvin pick acorns. Beauty is the idiot's consolation prize, she thought, yearning to switch faces and bodies with Fran. At least I have good hair, Paulina thought. If one focused on her hair, her features were charming, but when her hair was matted from the shower, her face looked belabored, like one of Milo's bad clay sculptures.

Paulina was so absorbed in Fran's crying that she didn't realize it was raining. Raindrops stuck in the girls' hair, puffing out their curls. Hairs that previously belonged to a curl, now stuck out mindlessly on their own. Fran sat in the wet grass, hunched like an old person.

"Is this part of your fantasy?" Paulina chided. "That he'll come back and pity you and carry you into his house like an abandoned kitten and take off baby's wet clothes and . . ." Fran pressed her ears closed as Paulina continued.

When the crying waned, Fran told herself that she was ugly, she was useless, and the crying came back. The crying felt like her final friend. The only thing she could do. Like she was good at it. She felt a terrible untethering from the world.

She didn't expect Julian, was no longer waiting for him, but couldn't motivate herself to rise. Fran felt the tiny hope that Paulina could help her. That however bad Fran felt, Paulina could reverse it if she wanted to. *You're so stupid*, Fran told herself, *that's so stupid*, and a new batch of tears came through, warming her cheeks, dripping from her nose.

Fran's crying soothed Paulina. Julian was nowhere. He must be working on his film, Paulina thought again. She'd never seen his work before. She hated student films. Student films disgusted her. But she would sit through it. Whatever thing it was. She would find him in the Film Building. She would claw through the recently weaned *anime* kids. Maybe it had to do with her, even, the movie. Maybe it was clearly about her, and everyone else was too stupid to realize it. Maybe it was good.

She felt drawn to Fran and repelled by Fran. She felt superior to all women and started walking quickly away from Fran. Houses of nonlovers blurred together as she passed. Lives that wouldn't touch hers. Lives she could touch, but didn't feel like it. She felt her old power collecting around her. She would watch this film. She would take Julian back to her place and let Fran drown in tears. Crying Fran was like the girls from her junior high who wore fairy wings—theater rejects in the grass.

Yet Fran hung out in her head like *Spirit of the Forest* or whatever. What was *Spirit of the Forest*? Where had she heard that? A beetle flew around her and landed in her hair. Beetles never know where they're going, Paulina thought, annoyed, swatting at it. Beetles know not what they do.

As she approached campus, she passed huddled groups of her classmates and paid them no mind. What the fuck were they whispering about? *Her?* Art students are so dramatic, she thought, weaving around them. She wasn't like them. She was a scholar. God, no, scholar sounded so stuffy and tweed and blah. She was one of the great thinkers of her time.

"Paulina!" Sadie was running toward her. Paulina kept walking. It was so like Sadie to cut short Paulina's glory with her kid-sister insistence. Julian was probably alone in the editing room, and the editing rooms locked.

Sadie's eyes were full of tears. "Wait, I have to talk to you," Sadie said, her face soggy. "Eileen died."

"Died?" Paulina asked.

"Yes. It's so awful. The whole thing is mysterious. I lent her my car last night and she was found . . ."

Paulina stopped and let her mind run. Eileen bought drugs from Fluff, a maniac who could not be trusted. A number of times Paulina had come close to trying heroin with Fluff at Mystic's warehouse, but always some force kept her back. She pictured Fran in the jumper at Mystic's and Julian taking it off her.

"At first she was in a coma, but by the time I heard about

it—" Sadie started crying again. "If only I hadn't lent her the car, or if I had gone with her, or, I don't know. I invited her to hang out with me and Allison, but I could have been more . . . I don't know . . ." She trailed off and Paulina watched her sink into the frivolous hoards of her mind.

"Oh, it's not your fault. That much is clear," Paulina said and gave Sadie a hug.

"I know, that's what everyone says, but it's not getting through to me," Sadie said, trembling. Paulina sat on the Foundation Building steps with Sadie, and listened to her tearfully cycle through the same thoughts. The longer Paulina lingered with Sadie, the more likely it was that Julian had finished his work and was walking to his apartment, discovering the crying mess on his lawn.

An hour later, the same phrases kept coming out of Sadie's mouth—*too young*, *my fault*, *no God*, *senior year*. Paulina could hear snippets of the other conversations around them, whispers of *drug party* and *death wish*. The next few weeks would be this same conversation over and over, she knew. She would sometimes have to manufacture the emotions. It would overshadow all the year-end parties.

Paulina squeezed Sadie's hand. "I wish I had more time to talk now," Paulina said. It was a relief to say this. Allison would come out from wherever, Paulina reasoned. She could leave now.

"Are you listening to me? Eileen has died. She will never return. She was one of us!" Sadie yelled.

"I wasn't as close to her as you were," Paulina said softly. "I wish it hadn't happened."

"She was nice!" said Sadie.

"Was she painting, or textiles or something?" Paulina asked looking at the Film Building in the distance.

"Textiles," Sadie said. "She had a good spirit."

"Well, good, because she's all spirit now."

"You're horrible!" Sadie said.

"I'm sorry," Paulina said.

Paulina wore a tight, dark dress to Eileen's service. She was having one of the best hair days of her life. A ringlet fell into her eyes, and she gently brushed it aside, careful not to ruin her eye makeup. It was truly tragic, Paulina knew. Eileen had lost everything! But still, Paulina was jealous of the love and attention she was receiving. The service was in the small park where students liked to go at night, pretending they were in a real city, drinking and freaking out over the moon.

If Paulina had to die one day, as every woman had before her, she liked to think her funeral would outdo this one in elegance and expense. There would be swans, and celebrities, and a river of tears. The gods would hover. Horns would sound. Just a glimpse of this eventual funeral left Paulina feeling ill. No event, no matter how impressive, could diminish the loss of Paulina's existence. Tears filled Paulina's eyes and she dedicated them to Eileen. Poor Eileen. If anyone wrote her biography, it would be very short.

Paulina scanned the rows of crying girls and saw Fran staring back at her with hatred. Fran was wearing a low-cut dress. She was sitting with the creatures from the Film Department, but one could see that even they didn't claim her as a friend.

The ceremony droned on and on. Sadie spoke. Allison spoke. Julian was nowhere to be found. Paulina checked her watch. Apollo sat down next to her. Paulina nodded in Fran's direction.

"What?" Apollo said.

"Her outfit," Paulina said. "Poor taste for a funeral."

"The funeral is actually on Sunday. It's family only. This is just the service."

Marissa turned around to shush them. Paulina stifled a laugh and Apollo nudged her. She laughed into his shoulder and tried to recall what it was that she always recalled to keep from laughing uncontrollably in lecture. Instead she recalled what kept her from crying in public—her high school boyfriend smearing his lips with what he believed to be Chap-Stick, but was really lipstick. She covered her smile. People cried. Paulina felt Fran's eyes on her and just let them burn.

She wished it were Fran's funeral. Julian would be there, and Paulina would sit next to him, their legs touching. She wondered what she would say at the podium with Fran listening behind the clouds.

Paulina grew restless. Everyone kept giving sad little toasts. People walked up to the microphone with no planned remarks, then talked about the cereals Eileen ate and the inside jokes she'd shared with her roommates. One hinged on the phrase "rumstick," which meant nothing to Paulina, but just hearing the word made two of the crying girls giggle helplessly.

While everyone gave their condolences to Eileen's family, Paulina sat with Apollo in the grass, dreaming up her funeral speech for Fran. She could imagine her older self standing before a small group of insignificants, noting Fran's hair, her dancing, imitating her lisp, but then Paulina's tone would change, retelling how Fran foolishly sold their friendship for a boy, and the crowd would cry. Then Paulina would sit back down next to Julian and politely wait until they were alone to have sex together, in honor of Fran, or maybe to spite her. Julian would propose to her after, and probably he'd be proposing to her all the time. She'd wave him off for his own good, because no man could ever make her happy for very long, she reasoned.

9

Fran searched her studio for the Whitney fellowship paperwork. The big room was empty of everyone except Fran, Gretchen, and a short antisocial girl named Marie, who painted in a photorealistic way her classmates publically dismissed but secretly admired.

"Eileen is gone forever," Gretchen said glumly.

"I know, it's crazy. Remember her freshman year? She used to hang out in her pajamas playing the guitar."

Gretchen wiped away tears. Fran spoke to Julian in her mind. It really was only a kiss, she insisted to herself. She watched Gretchen examine her paintings from the semester, which hung off thumbtacks on the wall. Gretchen offered no encouragement, not even a *hmm* of acknowledgment. Were they that bad? Gretchen wordlessly glided from one painting to the next as if they were in a gallery and the artist was as far away and unknown as a bright spot in the sky. Triumphantly, Fran found the fellowship application.

"Are you going to Eileen's party?" Fran asked finally, breaking the silence.

"It's not a party," Gretchen said firmly, "it's a celebration of life."

"Do you think Paulina will be there?" Fran asked.

"Everyone will be there."

Sampson's office was decorated with paintings by alumni, some of them semifamous painters who occasionally took the train up to critique student work. These guest crits were often more insulting than class crits. One woman told Fran that painting wasn't her medium.

Fran surveyed the paper clutter and pictures, Sampson's framed degrees on the wall, wondering if she would make it as far as him, or if she'd make it further.

"Fran, good to see you," Sampson said. His gaze fell on the form in her lap, covered with her careful handwriting. He smiled sadly behind his desk. "Oh, I'm sorry, dear. It was due weeks ago. I stopped by your studio but you were never there." Fran was stricken. "I even sent you an e-mail. I ended up asking Allison to apply instead. She was thrilled. It didn't seem you were too interested."

Fran burst into tears.

"Oh, Fran, you'll be okay. There are other fellowships out there." Sampson paused. "Maybe not as prestigious as this one, of course."

"I'm just sad about Eileen."

"A tragedy," said Sampson. "I just saw her work in the gallery. There's someone who could have made it."

Fran wiped her tears away. Where would she live? How would she make money?

"It's hard to be your age. There's maybe too much freedom. Or too much pressure . . ." He studied her.

She felt she had to say something, anything, but nothing came out. Sampson tapped a pen against the table. He had a wife and kids, but it was known he'd slept with Gilbert & George in the seventies. He smiled at Fran. "I really enjoyed that trip to Norway we took last year. That was something special."

Fran nodded.

"It was a joy to see you and that other girl, that bossy one. The sight of you two always gave Nils and me a kick. You were wearing those matching striped—what were they?"

"Tunics."

"Yeah, that's right." He laughed. Paulina had bought them a pair of striped tunics for twenty kroner at an Oslo market. It was too cold to wear them outdoors, but they'd done it anyway. "I'd be happy to write you a letter of rec," Sampson said. "You can use it for jobs or grad school or anything you want."

They'd made such a great pair that trip. Fran hadn't worried about school, or art, or her future. When she made Paulina laugh, she'd felt a golden light upon her. The light had formed a layer she thought to herself. The layer had been a kind of shield. She'd lost some kind of shield! And Julian's shield!

Fran tried to smile as she stood up and shook Sampson's hand. Perhaps painting wasn't her medium. The school had helped her see that. She had paid them to tell her. Fran walked outside into the cool spring air. She could feel the wet lines of her tears. Nothing was shielding her.

Arriving drunk to Eileen's party, Fran sensed Paulina, then saw her across the room with her back turned. The textiles girls looked radiant from mourning. A few people danced to loud music. "This is lame," Gretchen said, grabbing Fran's arm. "Eileen would want people to dance. Fran, you should dance. You love dancing."

"I don't feel like dancing. I'm not a machine. I can't just dance." She looked pointlessly for Julian. Julian never went to parties, or even to Artist Ball or the good lectures, but still Fran stared at the door, wishing for him. Sometimes she went into the cafeteria thinking she'd see him, but she never did. The cafeteria was always packed with freshmen and sopho- mores who didn't know her, having their own experience of the school without her.

"Did you figure out what you're going to do after gradu- ation?" Gretchen asked. Fran ran her fingers over the straps of her jumper. "Do you wanna live together in Brooklyn?" Gretchen asked. "You never said. It could be cool. I've been e-mailing people about apartments." Fran watched Paulina argue with Sadie. Allison was wilting against the wall. Sadie was holding hands with a boy Fran had never seen. "Jeez, you're like a zombie tonight," Gretchen said.

Everyone from their year was at the party. There was even a little pack of grad students who had probably been Eileen's TAs. No one felt right about dancing, but the music kept calling them to dance. "You don't need to decide now," Gretchen said, "but I just want to tell you that I'm definitely moving to New York, and as of now I don't have a roommate. I might rent an apartment starting June first, but maybe July first. August seems too late. I want to get on with the next part of my life. You know?"

Fran murmured in agreement. She watched as Paulina pantomimed something to a crowd. She must be making fun of someone, thought Fran. "Don't look now," Gretchen said and Fran turned to look. Julian stood self-consciously in the doorway. Fran's heart leapt. She missed his body, what it felt like to waste the whole day together. Julian was wearing black jeans and a Film Department T-shirt that read REEL LIFE. His thoughts briefly seemed visible as he looked everyone over.

"Dance with me," Fran whispered to Gretchen, then threw herself onto the dance floor. Gretchen watched her go. For a few supernatural moments, Fran was alone on the floor and captivating. Paulina was infuriated with inspiration. She threw her purse over her shoulder and walked her red leather boots onto the dance floor.

Julian stood silently while everyone else cheered them on. Paulina shook her breasts violently at Fran. Fran danced desperately low to the ground, as was supposed to be attractive. Paulina knew that the better dancer would win Julian. She sped up her moves. Her arms whipped the air. Her sight blurred.

Fran took a risk and started dancing slow. She let the beats pile up around her. Did she look good? She found herself praying to Eileen for help, but that was ridiculous, she knew—Eileen had just gotten there, she couldn't do anything yet. Paulina was vibrating in front of her. Fran spun away in a few wide, sensual movements. She felt a cramp dig into her side, but kept dancing.

The song ended. Paulina and Fran stood hunched, breathing hard. Paulina bent her knee in a stretch. They had barely recovered when Marvin walked in. No one had seen him for weeks. He'd cut his own hair. The next song came on. Paulina immediately resumed dancing. Fran reluctantly danced. Paulina danced at double speed, her breasts rocking an extra beat. The girls danced close together in a sexy way, but it only made Marvin laugh.

The old Color Club song came on, and Paulina and Fran danced even closer. Their eyes met and neither looked away. The music was an electronic whine, machines confessing to machines. Everyone ran onto the dance floor. Fran could feel the sweat on her back and between her breasts. She danced limply, like laundry on a line. She could feel the others dancing around her. She heard their tinny voices in the lyric breaks, and several spirited screams.

Fran's hair was in her eyes and she braided it out of her way as she danced. The cramp had faded, or the natural drug of dance had cured her. They'd called it "dance drugs" in Norway. They didn't run out of moves. They kept making up new ones. A happy heat emanated off their skin.

Paulina watched Fran's hair curl out of its braid and whip her face like pretty underwater plants. Paulina could not leave beauty alone. She leaned close to Fran. Fran was unable to resist anyone who wanted her. They kept an inch between their lips, while the room shook with dancing. The anticipation was so overwhelming that Fran couldn't tell who it was, but one of them leaned forward. The kiss was dizzying.

Like most bathrooms at school, there was dirt between the tiles. A discolored shower curtain clung to the tub. A bar of soap sat in a milky puddle. Someone knocked loudly on the door and Paulina locked it. She pulled Fran's jumper off, ripping a big hole in the seam. Laughing, Fran pulled Paulina's dress over her head.

Fran's bra was the flimsy kind with no underwire. Her breasts were soft and palmable. Every part of her told Paulina something, something she'd already known but never felt. Someone knocked again and Paulina yelled, "Get lost!" Fran started kissing Paulina again, this time with confidence. Her hands crushed Paulina's impossible curls and felt the hair clips beneath it all.

Paulina pulled Fran onto the floor, where she lay short of breath, staring at the rusted underside of the sink, someone's lumpy bathrobe, and a collection of half-full shampoo bottles. Paulina dragged Fran's threadbare underwear down her legs.

Fran had this bedroom feeling to her, a feeling Paulina had often noticed. Everywhere Fran went, she inhabited like her bedroom. Her joy, her moping—none of it was hidden. Paulina pressed her cheeks against Fran's thighs. Fran felt herself dissolve into the mess around her. Hot blood coursed through her veins, which she imagined like thin streets that led her to Paulina. To Paulina's streets.

Fran's melodic gasps tightened Paulina's heart. Emotions thrashed around like toys. Though it lasted about eight minutes, the girls would think of this moment so often that it became notched in their memory, a place they got stuck thinking. Hearing Fran orgasm drove Paulina insane. After, Fran reached for her, but Paulina evaded her. Cool fear filled Paulina while Fran lay catching her breath. Pleasure ran druggy sprints down Fran's legs. She couldn't think. Everything she thought seemed marvelous. She laughed.

Paulina washed her face in the sink, her heart pounding. Fran leaned against the door. "What about you?" Fran said. "I can get you," she said, her breasts lolling on her chest. "I want to." Paulina didn't respond. She dressed quickly, then nervously took out her hair clips and redid her hair, staring hard at her own face.

"Paulina!" A boy called through the door. Fran's mind raced. What would people think when they left together? How could she get the ripped jumper back on? Safety pins? What about Eileen? *Where was she?*

Then again, "Paulina!"

Paulina silently unlocked the door and closed it behind her. Fran looked for her underwear. Her legs felt weak, as though Paulina had stolen her power.

Fran held her ripped jumper closed as she walked away from the party. Where had Paulina run off to? Things could be like Norway again. Fun like that. In the same room. Going places together. Where the street split, Fran took the turn to Paulina's. Her shoes eagerly slapped the pavement. She touched her hair. She imagined finding the door open, sneaking into Paulina's bed. Paulina waking and finding her. What happened in the bathroom happening again and again.

Fran passed a weird sculpture glued to the sidewalk. It was the letter *E*, sculpted in papier-mâché, but the top bar had collapsed onto the other bars, and ants were eating it. Metal pieces hung off the sculpture with string. Photographs had been glued onto the piece: pictures of Eileen weaving on a loom, blurry dancing, Dean in a dress at the goth club with Sadie, freshman-year Marvin posing with naked Apollo, Eileen helping Cassie paint her room. Fran searched them for herself.

Paulina knelt above Tim in her bedroom, giving him the longest blow job in human history. "I told you," Tim said, bunched against her pillows. She waved him off.

"If anyone can do it, I can do it," she said, her words garbled. They laughed. Paulina worked like a motor. There really is no other feeling like this, she thought. It felt like praying to a needy god or resuscitating a drowned toad. She could think of nothing to drive her forward except the distinction of breaking his record. She pictured Fran and kept going. Fran's orgasm had sounded so sweet. She could picture a whole life with Fran. A sunny apartment, where, Berlin? She kept her hand moving up and down Tim's dick, while she stretched her neck.

"You can stop if you want," he said. She narrowed her eyes

and put it back in her mouth. Cassie couldn't give him a blow job! Cassie, who'd spent her whole artistic worth on a droopy monument for Eileen. Tim groaned.

"It feels so good, but I know I'm not going to come," he said, with a little too much certainty. Paulina sped up. She pictured Fran on the bathroom tiles with her legs open. Fran on the dance floor with her hair flying. Paulina had gotten all of Smith to come; surely Tim's dick wasn't as complex. Muscles in her back seized up like armor. She imagined leaving Tim in her bed and running to Fran's. Likely it had already ended for Fran, she realized. Fran rarely questioned a good feeling, but by now she had realized who had given it to her, and probably she wanted her lovers to be male, and of a certain look, of a certain major. A lot of Smith was this way. College girls intuit that they're supposed to try something while they're young, but rarely can they love or accept it. Likely Fran was already at Julian's, telling him, having him.

She let it fall out of her mouth. "I sucked Tim Henley's dick for four hours and all I got was this stupid T-shirt?" she said. He laughed. "I chased Tim Henley all year and all I got was this stupid blow job!?"

"Hey," he said, getting serious, "you started it."

Fran knocked, but the sound yielded nothing. She saw a pinkish glow from the window of Paulina's room. Fran wanted to yell to her, but she didn't want Paulina's neighbors to hear. She heard laughter and shrank back. Was Paulina looking at her through the blinds? Was it all a joke?

Fran had so much work to do, and here she was, shivering in the night, while Paulina laughed her villainous laugh. Was there a sorrier state? Paulina had won, had worn Fran down, had all Fran's power. Was Julian up there too? She felt sick. Wind flew through her ripped jumper. She wanted to scream to Paulina. "Paulina," she said. Light played in the window. If Paulina really liked her like that, Fran thought, it wouldn't have taken this long. When Paulina wanted someone she walked toward them, put her hands on them. Fran's eyes were glassy with tears and yearning. She couldn't yell. "Paulina," she said to herself.

10

A week later, they all graduated in faux silk, then, like trash in the water, floated off to lousy jobs in obscure towns and heartless cities. Terrible things happened in the news. People killed one another in inventive ways, and Fran read about it guiltily, as if her interest promoted it.

Fran hadn't expected to move to Upstate New York, but it was satisfying to paint houses. It felt human to trust ladders. It was the only job that responded. She'd gotten the call the same day she applied, and had accepted the offer before finding Hudson on a map. She'd be in nature! Or near nature.

She slept in the extra room of an old woman's house. The room had two windows, a small closet, and a sooty fireplace where spiders traveled long distances to die. Fran used the fireplace as an altar for her one love letter from Julian and a student evaluation from Sampson. She looked to these little papers in the dark, evidence that she could impress people.

When Ruthie had showed her the house, Fran was so charmed by her quick wit and wise eyes that she hadn't looked at the other apartments on her list. Fran imagined the old woman telling her life story over glasses of wine. Fran saw herself spiritually reviving the old woman, perhaps somehow encouraging a love affair between Ruthie and an old (but handsome) mailman or neighbor, and this successful union would be so emotionally satisfying that Fran wouldn't mind being single herself, having done this good deed. These fantasies vanished once Fran moved in. It seemed Ruthie had saved all her energy and good spirits for that first meeting and now she returned to her normal state of reading the newspaper and forgetting she had water boiling. Nights, Ruthie slept in front of the television surrounded by a haunted civilization of dolls, figurines, and fake flowers.

As Fran tiptoed around Ruthie, she thought of her fellow graduates trying new drugs, seeing old bands, taking the road trip people took from one part of California to another. Weekends she took herself to the local bar, Gruff's, dressed like she was still at school, waiting to be discovered. If Paulina were here she thought, we'd make friends with the old men playing Hearts, we'd flood the jukebox with Bowie and buy each other weird drinks—but Paulina had left her in the bathroom.

At the Lanfers' house, which they were painting a very dark blue, she threw the tarp off the ladder and sat waiting for the others. The company was run by an angry old man. The other painters were men in their thirties and forties. They smoked and had tanned, worn skin. On break they all ate sandwiches in the shade. It felt very American to Fran.

She spoiled good days calling Julian's old number and hearing the robot woman's voice—*the number you are trying to reach is no longer in service, please try again*. Only *I* could be jealous of a computer's voice, she thought. She had no one to talk to. She was friends with Allen and Pete at work, but they didn't *hang out*. No one went to the farmer's market with her. She walked there herself.

At school she'd seen herself as special, but in the weeks since graduation the world had slowed and now it was clear that everyone was as insignificant as the scrappy backyards one passes on trains. Forget style or talent; now it seemed the best thing a person could have was a house. One bought a house and then chose a color. The first house Fran helped paint was purplish gray, a ghostly, nuanced color. A woman on Franklin Avenue picked a fiery orange. One chose a color and a lover. One found a lover and trapped them with love.

"Are you coming?" Gretchen asked, her familiar voice breaking through the cocoon of Fran's new life—the faint crackling of a record at the end of its side, a foreboding smell that filled the kitchen whenever Fran or Ruthie opened the fridge.

"That's why I'm calling," Fran said. "I can't. I paint too slow. I have to work today."

"But it's a holiday!"

"I know. I can hear firecrackers down the street. But I gotta go to the Lanfers'." Fran wondered if Gretchen was mad. A box fan blew from her window. "The guys I paint with call me Snail," she said. "Isn't that cute?" Talking to Gretchen, new Brooklyn Gretchen, Fran had to root hard for herself, convince herself that *she* was the interesting one, *she* was the artist. Julian had loved *her*, might still love her. She could hear people where Gretchen was, people laughing. "Where are you?"

"I'm at the party. I'm on some guy's roof. Some guy James knows. It's really fun. People are comparing tattoos. A bunch of kids from school are going to come by later."

Fran looked out her bedroom window where Ruthie was watering the plants with a big rusted can. "What do you even do out there?" Fran asked, knowing.

"Branding. Web design." There was a long pause in which Fran could hear a female voice calling plaintively for ice. "Are you making paintings?" Gretchen asked.

"Tons," Fran said, looking at her blank wall. Nights she lay on her futon, daring herself to paint, afraid the painting would be bad. "There's an old barn where they let me paint." This sounded plausible but wasn't true. Fran could hear Gretchen talking to someone. "Who is that?" she asked. "Someone from school?"

"It's hard to hear you. It's really crazy here. Everyone's been drinking all day. Just move here. You can stay with me until you get a job. We'll hang out. We'll have fun." Fran heard music and more talking on Gretchen's end. It sounded like Gretchen had grown prettier to the world. Fran pressed Ruthie's landline receiver to her face. It smelled like saliva from the eighties.

"Well, thanks. I might do that sometime. But I don't like crowds. Plus Paulina," Fran said. "I don't want to see her."

"I haven't run into her once," Gretchen said, losing patience. "New York isn't the size of a room."

"Remember when *you* hated Paulina?"

"I overreacted," Gretchen said. "I didn't like being mad at Andrew, so I took it out on her."

Gretchen itched to get off the phone. Freshman year, Fran had been the loveliest, most interesting person Gretchen had ever met. They used to lie on the grass and Fran would captivate her with stories and non sequiturs. Now she sounded more like a runaway teen than a promising artist.

"You talked about her endlessly!" Fran exclaimed.

"Yeah, but I got over it."

There was so long a pause that Fran wondered if Gretchen had forgotten about her.

"Did you ever remember your e-mail password?" Gretchen asked suddenly.

"Yes, and I wrote it down. But I still don't own a computer."

The Internet isn't just a fad, you know, Gretchen had once told her in the Computer Lab. Now she just said, "Okay, well, gotta go, talk soon, bye."

Fran daydreamed about the party (audacious colors, music dug up from a time capsule). She imagined moving to New York, walking with Gretchen, some man running into her and her slides falling on the ground, the man holding them up to the light . . .

Fran's paintings show a wonderful mastery of color, light, and form. This semester's work benefited from her decision to stop painting from photographs, and instead draw from the vivid pictures in her mind. The result is a brilliant skewing. In these pieces, life is slanted and disproportionate. Humans look demonic and unreal. Without details to copy, Fran's lines and washes render emotions through texture. The color palette is completely unexpected. Should she continue in this path, she will find herself far beyond her original skills.

She could recite it. She stood in the shower washing the paint from her skin, thinking, *The result is a brilliant skewing.*

At her desk, Fran sketched the faces of the house painters she spent her days with, but the drawings looked cartoonish. She scribbled over them with her expensive art pencil. She smoked the wimpy clump of weed she'd bought off Allen and lay down on the floor.

The world was relaxing and rejoicing. She rolled over and did two pushups. The world was having sex and getting drunk. She lay naked on her bed, but was too bored to masturbate. She imagined this written on a T-shirt: TOO BORED TO MASTURBATE. Or maybe: 2 BORED 2 MASTURBATE. She imagined selling the shirt to Spencer's and Hot Topic, getting rich. She knelt by the fireplace.

Dear Fran,

You are in class right now. I am sitting in your bed. Your room is filthy! There are mountains of clothing. . . .

She folded the letter back up. Tonight is the night I dance at the bar, she told herself. No matter what music is playing. And everyone will get up and dance with me. I will meet the kids who squat in the warehouse. She searched her closet for something to represent her.

At the bar, she danced to classic rock songs with a crew of drunken girls who wore gold hoop earrings and bras that thrust whatever breasts they had high into the night. "I would kill for your hair!" one of the girls told her. Another yelled,

"I'm Annie!" in her ear. There was a good ten minutes of ca-
thartic dancing. The girls applauded Fran's flamboyant moves,
accepting her into their group. Fran felt a rush from this, but
soon discovered that the girls were only performing for the
men at Gruff's. These men, unshaven and cloaked in flannel,
clutched their beers and made no motions toward dancing.
Their eyes were locked on the TV.

Lying in bed, waiting for sleep, a circus of thoughts flashed
within Fran. She would make new paintings and get her paintings in the town library, and then in a coffee shop, and then
in a . . . She didn't like the galleries in town. She would start
a gallery in a shack and then move it . . . She would become a
realtor. She would travel to Haiti—no, to Egypt—and a man
would approach her and be Julian.

Fran could hear the voices of the visiting artists from her
painting classes telling her to move to New York City. One
couldn't be a real artist out here, they insisted. One *might*
flourish upstate, but only after making it in the city. She had
to go to galleries, she knew. She had to suffer, and do her suffering in the right place.

Sadie and Allison had ignored Paulina's calls after graduation,
forcing her to get an apartment in New York with a pregnant
stranger. No one Paulina wanted to see would see her. Instead she got drunk with bores. Her style was wasted on those

around her. Hustling down Midtown streets with a crowd of strangers, she would crack and start telling the others how to live. There was a better New York she'd read about, and she saw it in short moments that excluded her. A crazy man dressed all in white, with tight pants, shiny white shoes, and gold jewelry winked at her, and she felt he was magic or special, that he had something to say. But when she crossed the street toward him, he screamed at her.

She'd heard that Fran was in New York too, and for the first few weeks she stepped onto every train with grace, thinking Fran would be watching. They'd graduated a few names away from each other, but hadn't spoken since the bathroom orgasm. Paulina moped among the racks in overpriced vintage stores. She got a job at a discount shoe store, then discovered Renaldo's, where she worked for months before the incident.

Renaldo's was an old, updated saloon with the best Italian food in Queens. A long bar lined one side and the ceiling was gold tin. It was the first place in the city that moved Paulina— that resembled the secret New York she'd dreamed of. "In a past life I frequented here," she'd told the bartender her first night. Later, when a fight broke out in the party room, Paulina excitedly clutched at the flocked wallpaper. She returned the next day with her résumé and met Renaldo himself.

Eventually Renaldo was forced to fire her, but she didn't

blame him. She blamed Philip. His teasingly lean physique. His hands in suds. His apron ties falling untied. She'd had little effect on him. At first he answered her questions and listened to her, and Paulina felt an electric attraction between them. She dressed more and more provocatively and bought him drinks after their shift. She tried to respect his shy manner, but started to suspect it was just another sex game.

She played the game. She bought him a record—he said he liked records—and waited for him to take her up on her offer, but eventually he ceased all communication, even when she snuck away from her stand to keep him company in the kitchen. By then, she could wait no longer, and boldly showed him what he was missing.

Paulina much preferred Renaldo's Queens apartment to her own. It was decorated with sports memorabilia. She liked the smoky smell. The cracks between the floor slats were filled with crumbs and bits of paper. "You look like someone who does scratch-off tickets," she'd told him after she got the hostess job.

"Desperate?" he'd asked, surprised.

"Local," she'd said.

Renaldo didn't condone her actions. What she had done to Philip was wrong. If a man had done that to a woman, Renaldo would have turned the man in. But she entertained him. After he fired her, she'd pleaded with him for work, and for a short while she worked the books for him, until it was discovered she'd been shortchanging Philip. Renaldo was still sore about it, but by then he was sleeping with her. She'd made herself a key one day while he was in the shower, and hung around his house like the last guest at a party.

"If you even kiss that girl, she'll never leave you alone," his friend Andy warned him one night as they smoked outside the restaurant.

Renaldo agreed. There was something unstable about Paulina, like a top, or a wrecking ball.

"You've already fucked her, haven't you?" Andy laughed. Renaldo looked off toward the Queensboro Bridge in the distance. "Stop me when I get ahead of myself. Has she already moved in?"

Renaldo stayed quiet. Andy scoffed at him. It was Andy who had pulled Paulina off Philip, while the cooks laughed and hit their pans.

Fran sat on Gretchen's couch, tired from the bus, still picking the fiery orange paint off her leg. The week before, she'd spilled a paint bucket on the porch of the Franklin Avenue house. She'd stood stunned as it pooled and dripped onto the white trim Allen had just finished, then fell onto the flowers below, spotting them, coating them, then flattening them. "Oh, hell!" Pete had shouted. "Pick up the bucket!"

She'd spent a disastrous week chipping away the orange, sanding down the boards, and then repainting, knowing the whole time she'd be fired when she finished. Her boss took the damage costs out of her last paycheck. She hadn't cried, though, she reminded herself, surveying the boxes in Gretchen's living room. Gretchen was true to her promise and said Fran could crash at her place until she got a job. Fran opened a new Photoshop file on Gretchen's computer and wrote *Thank You!* in a silly font, but then erased the words, remembering how Gretchen criticized her when she'd said she didn't want to see Allison's show.

Fran struggled with her résumé in Word. She knew that Gretchen would be opposed to her use of borders, but Gretchen would never know. She had no phone herself, so she put down Gretchen's number. She applied for an artist assistant job in Chelsea and felt so certain she would get it that it seemed a waste to try for others, but she applied for two more. One was an art-handling job in Long Island City. That would be good, Fran thought. She'd get strong. Hopefully not *too* strong, she thought. The other job was a graphic design job. She'd just ask Gretchen what she didn't know.

Fran allowed herself to go through Gretchen's closet and try on her new clothes. While she was digging around, she saw a fancy wood box that probably hid a dildo or a scroll of confessions, but she wouldn't let herself open it. She found a drawing she'd given Gretchen at school—and Gretchen had *folded* it. Fran fumed. Graphic designers weren't *real* artists, she thought. They just made signs. They just made money. Fran opened the wood box and it was filled with jewelry. She slammed it shut.

When Renaldo got back from work, he found Paulina on the couch reading a magazine, as she'd been every day that week. "How's the new girl?" she asked.

"Fine. Good." He took off his work shirt and put on a T-shirt.

"I had a particular flair for the job though, wouldn't you say?"

"I've said as much myself," he said.

"If only you'd have let Philip go instead," she began softly. Renaldo laughed. "He's a tragic figure," Paulina said.

"That's what you say about your roommate," Renaldo said.

"Everyone is tragic." He stared at her ill-fitting dress. "It's too hot to fuck," she said. "If that's what you're thinking."

He shook his head. He'd known at first sight that he wanted Paulina for Renaldo's, but she'd been trouble from the beginning. She talked too much. Her attitude took up space. She had the condescending gaze of a palm reader.

"Am I tragic?" he asked her, pouring two glasses of whiskey from the bottle he kept on the counter.

"Hell yes," she laughed. "You are *middle-aged*, tragic in itself. You wanted a life of adventure, but you're stuck in Queens. You gamble half your money away and spend the rest on me, an overeducated drifter."

"But the restaurant," he said, smiling. He handed Paulina a glass and sat back in his worn leather recliner.

"The restaurant is great," she agreed.

"You don't know real tragedy. You're twenty-two. How could you?"

"I have always known tragedy," Paulina insisted and told him the life story she used as her own, the one that had horrified her years ago in the bus stop downtown. Renaldo listened, gently rattling the ice in his glass. It was a riveting, sickening story.

"None of that happened to you," he said afterward. "Where did you read that, in a book?" He reached over and finished her whiskey for her. Paulina pouted.

"Most of it happened."

He laughed. "Where are your parents really?"

"Dead, like I said." This part she'd almost convinced herself was true.

"Both in a plane crash?" he asked dubiously.

"One in the plane crash, the other in the boating accident," she said with stony eyes.

"Which one was in which?" he asked, amused.

"Does it matter?!" She looked off. She imagined flames. Flames and waves. She imagined herself standing over two serious graves.

Renaldo glanced back toward the payroll books on his roll-top desk. "By the way, it's official. I put Andy on accounting." He watched her face adjust. "It's nothing personal. You know I like having you around."

She looked at him with disdain. "It's too hot to fuck," she said. He shook his head. Andy was right. It was a real task to rid himself of her. With difficulty, she took off her dress and strutted over to where he sat hunched in his chair. She sat on his lap. Sexually, he found her exhausting. It was baffling that she wanted him. Girls her age usually avoided his eyes completely. She drew her face close to his.

For weeks, he'd been dreaming of a way to end things without hurting her pride, and now it came to him simply. "I'm getting too attached to you," he said into her neck. He ached under her weight. "I don't want you to see anyone else."

Paulina glowed from this victory. All month she'd camped out by his heart with little love of her own, but a stubborn need to star in someone's life.

She eyed his small apartment. By the front door was a cheap elephant statue where Renaldo kept his keys. There was a brown spot where the bulb had burned a hole in his lampshade. All of it could be hers: The king-sized bed. The mirrored drawers. The Southern accent he used for jokes. The pile of cop novels in his closet. The drooping Mets tattoo on his bicep. He winced under her weight, and she did not shift. "I think I . . ." His voice ventured out as if on a tightrope. Familiar dread enveloped Paulina, slowing her hearing. The fan sounded rickety. Everything felt flawed.

"I'm unable to love you back in a permanent way," she said. "I have a plan, actually many plans for myself, and none of them take place here." He nodded at her. Paulina felt a kind of momentum she had lacked for months. She transcended Renaldo's and Renaldo and the whole lazy affair she had orchestrated. She felt dangerously attractive to men and bloated with potential.

But, Paulina had no other place to go besides her buggy apartment. She despised the other young people in the city. She had no money. She didn't want to leave his lap. She pictured Philip's gray eyes. "Let's end this right," she said, throwing herself into a long, aggressive kiss. Renaldo kissed her back. *He loves me*, Paulina thought, and it made him seem weak to her. She fantasized his death, being the last woman he loved.

Fuck Philip, she thought, pulling off Renaldo's shirt. Fran would have wanted Philip. Might have gotten Philip. *Fuck Fran*. Paulina tugged at Renaldo's pants, then lay waiting on the couch. Renaldo stood and sighed, taking off his pants and underwear. *I'm fucking you, Philip*, she thought, and the thought echoed in the chamber of her body. *I'm fucking you, Fran*, she thought again and again and again until the words had no meaning. Afterward, she felt immense love for Renaldo. *He is unlucky to lose me*, she thought, and left him minutes later while he was in the bathroom.

The sublet ended when Danielle had the baby. The baby looked awful and red, but Danielle insisted that's how they were supposed to look. Without her scholarship's stipend, Paulina couldn't afford another apartment. She sold her clothes to the overpriced vintage stores she abhorred. She thought of her parents as the two serious graves. She imagined her hometown bombed out and boarded. She imagined a sad scrapbook of her parents' obituaries. She pictured herself pulling out this scrapbook and showing people. Renaldo coming across the scrapbook in his apartment. Renaldo being moved by the scrapbook. Renaldo laughing at the fake scrapbook.

Paulina pocketed muffins at bodegas. She found no glamour in the poverty she'd dreamed of as a child. She slept in the playgrounds of parks. She washed herself in the bathroom at Port Authority. Through it all, her hair looked impeccable.

"Hair is the outgrowth of the soul," she told a man at the bar. He laughed. She examined his glasses, his tie, his shoes. He started to tell a story involving a scandal in the finance world—a good sign. For the last week, she'd been sleeping in the art lofts in Bushwick. One boy would take her home; the next day she'd befriend his neighbor in the hall. The boys were less distracted than the warehouse guys from the art school, but their lofts were decorated the same way: stolen street signs, Christmas lights, Dr. Bronner's nonsense on the soap in the shower, bikes on the wall, unfinished projects taking up whole tables or rooms.

But tonight she wanted a nice apartment, someone who had to be up early for a job. Sometimes she sat in the corner of a bar, shyly looking at her hands like she'd been stood up by a date. She knew how to play pool so badly that men couldn't resist instructing her. Each man held a little promise for her— food, time, space.

In the middle of the night, she woke up in a high-rise apartment in Brooklyn Heights, then stayed awake, pretending she lived there. She made a messy omelet and devoured it. She looked for women's clothing in the spare closet. She showered and deep conditioned her hair. An *I Love Lucy* marathon comforted her. *Through it all*, Paulina wrote on the back of an issue of *GQ*, *I still think I will find—*

"What the fuck are you doing?" the finance guy asked, squinting in the doorway.

11

While nagging a hot dog vendor for a pretzel, Paulina smelled familiar perfume. The smell recalled the old, easy life of frolicking and looking at amateur drawings. Paulina turned and saw long black hair trailing away. "Sadie!" she exclaimed.

Sadie recoiled at the voice and walked faster. Midtown was crowded with businesspeople and mascots. A children's field trip filled the space between Paulina and Sadie. Construction workers were building the new MoMA. Sadie cut a corner. It was the worst time to be spotted. *My whole career depends on this interview*, she thought. She knocked an old woman off her feet as she passed, then gasped and knelt to help her up. Paulina watched. "Hey," Sadie said, flustered.

"At last! I've been trying to get in touch with you." Seeing Sadie revived Paulina's sunken spirits. Sadie was like a misplaced doll, triumphantly found.

"Really? I'm actually late for a job thing," said Sadie. She would not let herself say, *But I'll call you this week* or *But let's meet up for coffee*. She turned to go.

"Let's have a drink tonight," said Paulina.

"Tonight's not good," Sadie said. She slowly walked away and Paulina followed behind. Sadie glanced back. Paulina's curls were still so healthy and shiny! But other parts of her looked desperate and rundown. Her skin was dry in patches, her eyebrows unruly. Sadie was already mentally relaying the scene to her therapist.

"Is this about the boots? I'll give them back," Paulina said. Sadie kept walking. "Is it about Eileen still?" Paulina crossed herself. "I could have been more sensitive. Everyone does their own thing with death."

They wove around strangers on the sidewalk. Huge buildings shut them off from the sky. "What job thing?" Paulina asked. "How's that boy you're seeing?"

"Eric's good. We have a place together." Sadie had married Eric just the week before. She had designed her dress— long, blue, with peacock feathers. Only the best people Sadie and Eric knew were invited. Sadie saw no reason to curate the rest of her life any differently. She held her portfolio case with both hands. "This is where I have my appointment," she told Paulina in front of a black, mirrored tower.

"What kind of job?" Paulina asked. "I'm still looking too, if you can believe it. I've been hosting for a restaurant," she said self-consciously. "But I want something more regular."

"It's a fashion thing," Sadie said dismissively and walked into the lobby. Paulina followed her.

"I like fashion," Paulina said, adjusting her dress. Her voice echoed into the vaulted ceiling. Sadie checked in at the reception desk and was agitated when Paulina did the same.

They rode up the elevator together. "You need an appointment," Sadie said. "Plus you don't have a portfolio."

Paulina laughed. "I don't need a portfolio."

They sat on opposite ends of the waiting room. "What kind of company is this?" Paulina asked the boy next to her.

"Teenage girl stuff. Like Forever 21. There's this team of new investors in there looking to reinvent the company. A lot of money is sitting at that table!"

Paulina smiled at him and then Sadie, but Sadie wouldn't return her gaze. A few minutes with Paulina had completely dismantled Sadie's well-being. *Don't waste yourself on the past*, her therapist had stressed after a series of Paulina dreams. Paulina cutting Sadie's houseplants with scissors. Paulina sitting silently in Sadie's closet.

The therapist was one of the new things, along with the expensive black portfolio and referring to Eric as her husband. Sadie began a text to Allison that read: *Queen Pauline in Midtown, could not shake her, send help,* but she needed to focus on the interview; she watched the cursor delete her words. She looked to her phone for a picture of her and Eric that might repair her. The one from the rehearsal dinner. He looked handsome in that picture. There was a good future in his jawline. She had noticed this on the train, years before. The receptionist looked over her marble desk. To Sadie's dismay, Paulina's name was called.

Paulina gazed empty-handed at the formal, well-groomed people seated around the conference table. They looked at her expectantly. This was the kind of moment she had been preparing for. Her spontaneous ideas were better than most people's labored thinking, she told herself. She remembered the way the Venus Flytrap had sauntered over to Eileen's fish tank and grabbed Eileen's favorite fish.

Paulina ran her hand over her curls and was flooded with confidence. "Your clientele are easily convinced that wrapping a vintage tablecloth around them will win them true love. The operative word is vintage. Today's America is grimy and organized. There is none of the romantic languor of gourmet European farm towns. Teens want to look lazy and mysterious. Their clothes shouldn't tell you if they are rich or poor—it is tedious to be either. The clothes should hint at an adventure just taken place or about to unravel."

Paulina couldn't read the executives' faces. She continued.

"Give them vintage clothes without the stink of someone else's troubles. This is their golden time. Their boys are virgins. Their surroundings don't match their exuberance. They need the clothes and music to transform their habitat. They are trying out their personalities, some of them for the first time."

Paulina looked at a dry erase board where someone's careful drawing of a sports bra glowed from the projector. The executives stared at her. "What about for the men's line?" a man asked. His bald head and bushy eyebrows made him look distinguished. He wore a suit like the others and a flashy red shirt. "We might want to go in that direction," the man said. The others at the table shot him a look. Paulina paused to think. Her mind was as empty as an oven. Stray thoughts passed like birds.

"Is that a Halston?" the man asked. Paulina just stared at him. "Your dress," he said. "Who is it?"

Paulina clutched the ruffled SUPERTHRIFT dress, which she'd sold to Beacon's Closet and then stolen back.

"Oh, yes. Halston." The word sounded good in her mouth. She'd heard of that, of him, from *The Andy Warhol Diaries*. All her dresses were suddenly Halstons. The man smiled at her, while the others scrutinized her dress.

"If that's a Halston . . ." a woman started to say.

Paulina stepped forward. "Similar for the men," she said. "Relaxed and brawny. Like they're coming back from the duck hunt to meet your parents at a restaurant. Like they're on a solo graffiti mission while everyone else is taking their SATs. Graphic silkscreens, distressed denim, but add some lining, trim, piping. Let the girls and boys continually one-up each other." The projector moved of its own accord, the sports bra was replaced by a fitted tank top.

"What is your design experience?" a woman asked.

"It's limited. I don't see myself designing as much as curating. I have a fantastic sense of predicting and creating trends."

"May I ask what products you use on your hair?" asked the man in the red shirt.

"It's something I've invented. I'd tell you the ingredients, but my business manager wants me to resist until I get a patent." *Business manager!* Paulina reveled at her quick thinking.

"I think we're done here, Harvey," one of them said. Someone sighed. The group's focus broke, and all at once they turned to one another, talking and checking their phones, drinking from the bottles of water that lined the table, opening and closing their laptops. If Paulina had surprised them, now they surpassed her. They had already forgotten her, though she still stood there, unable to leave.

The man reached over the table to give Paulina his card. "Regardless of what the board decides, I invest in beauty products and think we have common interests." The card burned in her hand. *Harvey Benizio.*

. . .

"But how did your interview go?" Allison asked Sadie, scanning the gallery. She was young to have a solo show, especially at such a big gallery, but she wore her usual clothes and was not nervous. She spotted Gretchen and Fran across the room and looked away.

"Bad. I was totally weirded out. I couldn't stop thinking about Paulina. What was she doing there? Why did they let her go before me?" Sadie noticed Gretchen and Fran too. "I hear Gretchen is making lots of money. And look, Fran is still wearing that—" Sadie hesitated. They laughed. "Wait, don't look at them. I never know what to say to her," Sadie said.

"It's too late," Allison said as Gretchen walked toward them.

Fran and Gretchen hugged Allison and Sadie. Fran listened to their polite catch-up, answering "Hudson" and "house painting" and "still looking" when they inquired. She felt they could tell she'd spent the last month on Craigslist applying to decorate cakes, shear sheep, paint faces, and deliver flowers. They could sense that she'd considered posing for photographs and then researched pepper spray. Then looked into police sketch training and tattoo artist training. She applied to so many postings that she couldn't remember them the next morning, and not a single one replied.

Fran swayed in place looking for Paulina. Important art

world people talked across the room and cool-looking kids their age drank and laughed, but no one seemed exciting. The kids looked so like her old classmates that at first Fran assumed it was them, but this group was cleaner and more stylish. They were Cooper Union graduates who'd spent their saved tuition money on designer sneakers and mopeds. Whereas Fran's classmates had a battered, psychedelic vibe, these ex-students had appropriated a trailer-trash, hillbilly look—the boys at least. The girls were dressed like new wave French philosophers. They already had jobs and studios. Each had his or her own look, and was slowly exposing the art world to it, stamping themselves in.

Fran was jealous of them, but it was a yearning jealousy. If the jealousy had a voice it might have sung, *Fuck you, posers! Seduce me and give me a job. Let us work side by side in the big studio building on Twenty-Seventh, or is it Twenty-Fifth? Do you know Dana Schutz? The painter Dana Schutz—do you know her e-mail address? Never mind, just take me home and dress me. Confess to me. Take me to your roof-deck or the roof-deck of your friend.*

Her desire to know them was overpowered by doubt and pride. What could they show her? They had never loved and sweated on the Color Club floor. They were part of the gallery, the gallery's moving parts, an ambiance of youth staring at the bright drips and smears on the big square canvases. *I love your paintings*, Fran was about to tell Allison, when a tall willowy woman came over to Allison and said, "I love your paintings, dear."

Allison turned to talk to her, leaving Sadie, Gretchen, and Fran to themselves.

"That's Adria Bennet," Sadie whispered. Gretchen gasped.

"Who?" Fran asked.

"This totally awesome artist from London." The boredom set in again. When Fran used to take breaks with the house painters, no one needed to say anything, but here in the gallery she was afraid of being boring, she was afraid Sadie was boring, but she had entirely nothing to say.

"Remember that figure model Apollo?" Fran ventured. The girls laughed and Fran felt a nervous release.

"He's doing really well as a musician right now," Gretchen said. "He opened for Gorgeous Cyclops at Webster Hall. My friend is doing the art for his album." Fran's hair felt dry. She self-consciously braided it out of sight.

Sadie saw people she knew and went to greet them. Fran read Allison's artist statement on the wall.

My work affects my relationships with people. A painting will change my relationship to my parents, even though the painting is completely abstract.

Fran panicked. "Remember Marvin?" Fran asked Gretchen. "What happened to him? Where did he go?" Gretchen was so tired of Fran that even a small inquiry like this physically annoyed her.

"Is that Paulina?" Gretchen asked, squinting.

"Where?" Fran turned. Gretchen motioned to the window.

"I thought I saw her, but it was someone else."

"What do you think will happen to her?" Fran asked.

"I think she'll just go man to man, hitchhiking the world. That's what Dean said."

"Maybe she'll end up with a woman," Fran said, blushing.

"She's going to be one of those old ladies who draws in fake cheekbones. She'll probably keep birds."

"Wait, when did you see Dean?" Fran asked in disbelief. Then a startling thing happened. A boy walked over and started to talk to Gretchen, first about her glasses, (Were they Selima Salaun?) (Fran was shocked to hear they were) and then they talked about Gretchen's job, and then the boy's job, and his Yaddo residency, and Gretchen's Ping-Pong skills, and then they drifted off toward the wine, leaving Fran in the center of the gallery with nothing to look at except Allison's paintings, while around her strangers laughed, and drank, and got on with their lives. The paintings were good in an infuriating way, a way Fran wasn't able to articulate to Sadie's husband. "You know they're good," he said. "I know they're good. Why do we have to know why?"

"But that was the whole point of our school," Sadie explained, and she and her husband laughed.

Fran went out to the sidewalk to look for Paulina. A group of adults crowded around a bulldog and a poodle, making baby talk. Two men stood smoking. "Did you guys see a girl my age out here? She's got dark curly hair . . . almost reddish."

"Sort of weirdly dressed and carrying on about something or other?" one of the men asked. Fran nodded excitedly. "Yeah, we saw her." Fran's heart leapt. "And fuckin' twenty more just like her." They laughed.

Most of the pay phones in the city were broken. The receiver had been ripped out or the whole console removed, exposing a mass of wires. Symbols were scraped into the glass enclosures, any remaining phone books shredded to bits. Paulina dialed Harvey's number from the last working pay phone in the East Village, her heart trembling with each ring. When his secretary (a terse, androgynous voice) said Harvey was unavailable, she said she'd call back.

Carrying her bag of essentials, Paulina hopped a turnstile into the subway and endured steel drum music all the way to Queens. Her red boots punished her every step toward Renaldo's. There, she loitered in the lot behind the kitchen until someone—the old cook this time—went out for a smoke. Shivering for effect, she asked him to dump some of the leftover food in a box for her, and promised this act would make him shine brightly in God's eyes (wherever He may be) and ensure that George ascended to heaven when his time came, that instead of cooking for others he would get to run his own restaurant up there. George refused, threatening to call Renaldo.

Distressed by the idea of Renaldo seeing her unwashed dress, Paulina ran off, her bag weighing her down like an anchor. After an hour of fruitless wandering, she shoplifted a premade sandwich from a bodega and devoured it in the weeds behind a nearby gas station, listening to the wind roll a crushed beer can over the pavement and teenagers bicker over a lost bet. On the subway back, she lay across three seats in low spirits. She ran through the rain to the Starbucks bathroom, where she sat on the toilet long after she was finished, ignoring the knocks and voices, then brushed her teeth with the tattered toothbrush she kept in her bag.

I had so much potential, Paulina thought as she looked for a spot to sleep in the park. *But I am renowned for nothing!* She moaned loudly, stirring the dealers from their benches. Two scuttled toward her in the darkness, trying to sell her drugs.

The next morning, when Harvey was again unavailable, Paulina read off the number of the pay phone to the secretary.

This time she added that it was *Urgent!* and that she'd be leaving the country very soon.

All day she sat in the phone booth, eating old croissants from the bakery across the street. Finally the phone rang. Paulina took a deep breath, smoothed her eyebrows, and answered it as professionally as she knew how, but it was a woman asking for Percy. Though men of all shapes and sizes walked by with briefcases and dogs, holding phones to their faces, smoking their cigarettes, Paulina insisted there was no soul in sight. When the woman kept chattering on, Paulina hung up.

She left the booth only to pee and get water. She watched birds peck at a pizza crust until it was just a few burnt crumbs. Every time the phone rang, it was the same woman. "I can see no man living or dead," Paulina said, tired of life.

"But Percy gave me this exact number!" the woman cried.

"What does he look like," Paulina asked. "In case he shows later."

"He's short and pale and has eyes like the devil, and he'll be drunk because Aggie doesn't care right for him—"

"Just give me your number," Paulina said. "I'll write it down."

The woman repeated her number twice, and Paulina said uh-huh after each digit, but did not write it down, did not care what became of Percy or anyone else. She slumped against the cold glass. She felt like a useless body of itches, pains, and wants.

She spent the night in the phone booth, awakened twice by crazy people who wanted the phone, and once by a cop with something to prove. Harvey didn't call. After a second day by the phone, she was dreaming of the old college town. Could she live in some unused studio, getting swipes off freshmen's meal cards? A hunched woman poked Paulina's bag with a stick. Paulina shooed her away.

12

Though Gretchen had outgrown Fran professionally and emotionally and now had more than a dozen friends she much preferred, she still spent an occasional hour or two with Fran if she showed up outside Gretchen's office after work. She still found relief looking at Fran's face—it truly was like a face from a painting, the eyes staring into thoughts, the mouth open slightly in the moment before or after speaking.

It had been more than a year since Fran moved out of Gretchen's apartment. While they inhabited the same space, Fran's life seemed to crawl by one minute at a time, as Gretchen waited for her to get an interview, and then an outfit, and then an apartment. You could at least do the dishes, Gretchen had thought every day she came home to find Fran lying stoned on the carpet with a T. Rex song on repeat. After Fran moved out, her life seemed to move at an accelerated pace. Every time they talked there was some boy or roommate or coworker taking up her thoughts, as it had been before with Julian and Paulina.

At a bar, Gretchen half listened to Fran's issues with her latest boyfriend, a psychology major who insisted on biking to Fran's Bushwick sublet and always arrived late, exhausted, and ranting about animal rights. Once Fran had taken him to a party at Gretchen's and he'd sat in a closet, reading the *New York Times* on his laptop. Before him she had been seeing a waifish sound recorder Gretchen had never met, but whose penis Fran had twice drawn for her on a napkin.

Since Fran made little money painting ceilings and walking dogs, while Gretchen landed client after client, Gretchen regularly paid for their meals and drinks, while Fran mumbled things about "getting a real job" and "taking whatever I can get." This time, when Gretchen was about to lay down her card, Fran stopped her and put down cash instead.

"Okay, so here's the real news," Fran said, nearly skipping toward the subway. "That career counselor got me an interview for a job writing test questions. I had it yesterday. I got it!"

"Congrats!" Gretchen said, truly startled at the news.

"I bet it will give me a lot of painting ideas."

"Really?" Gretchen asked, no longer hiding the doubt she so often hid by forcing her eyebrows straight and her voice even.

"Well, it's visual art test questions, so it's creative."

"Where is it?"

"Ohio."

"You'd leave all this for Ohio?" she asked, pronouncing the word like it was an ancient place no longer on the map.

"There are still people in Ohio. There are bars. I think there's even art in Ohio!" Fran was showing some of the old, senseless passion that Gretchen had forgotten. "Jim Dine is from Ohio. Jim Drain is from Ohio . . ."

"I know someone who fucked Jim Drain," Gretchen ventured.

They silently crossed the street.

"Yeah?" Fran waited for Gretchen to ask her more about the job, but Gretchen was covertly checking her phone. More and more often Gretchen chose the tiny world in her phone over Fran. She scrolled through the little pictures of the little people in the phone, her face lighting up with a ghost-white glow.

"I thought you'd be excited for me," Fran said, staring at a homeless woman sleeping under cardboard.

"You should be painting, not selling your soul," Gretchen said without looking up.

"Since when do you care about my paintings?" Fran asked, watching Gretchen drop the phone into her leather purse. "You know, I saw that drawing I gave you. You folded it."

"What? The one you were going to throw out anyway? The one I rescued? Does it have a sort of dog person licking an angel?"

"It was Marvin as a deity, I think," Fran said haltingly. It wasn't such an achievement, Fran admitted to herself, but folding a drawing was inhumane. This kind of moment was occurring more often between them. It was like the bending of a stick—a moment where one could push harder and finally snap the bond. Fran would feel Gretchen's view of love was callous, or Gretchen would challenge Fran's nostalgia for school, but always they let the disagreements die in silence, protecting the tradition of the friendship, though sometimes that was all it was. They saw each other because they saw each other. They saw each other because they'd seen each other.

But Fran was thinking of her new job now; she no longer cared about the drawing. Burn the past to light the future, she thought, though the words came from an unknown source. "Anyway, I've been packing and stuff. I'm excited." She pictured herself at a desk, in her own cubicle. She imagined a digital display of all her earnings—big red numbers climbing quickly, like the ones near Union Square.

Gretchen suddenly remembered the coat she'd once lent Fran, a Rebecca Taylor coat that was surely the most expensive item in Fran's closet.

"I don't know how my roommates will take it," Fran said thoughtfully. "I haven't told them yet because I wanted to wait until I really—"

"Can I have my coat back?" Gretchen asked. "I mean before you pack it up."

"What?" Fran searched her pockets for her MetroCard as they took the steps down to the L train. "Oh yeah, of course."

The donate/destroy pile took up half of her room. Boxes of plaid stockings, gold leggings, fringe-covered boots, a zip-up one-piece with racing stripes, a tinfoil crown, ribbons, garish SUPERTHRIFT purses, high school friendship rings, mix tapes from boys, depressing underground comic books, old art history handouts, and a globe that Marvin had painted black. "I won't need this stuff in Ohio," she told Gretchen, who pawed through the clothes without finding a single thing worth adopting.

"Yeah, all you'll need is a fleece and, like, a deli sandwich," Gretchen said, reunited with her coat.

"What's wrong with fleece?" Fran asked self-consciously.

"Nothing. It's just the opposite of fashion. It's a gateway drug to an unglamorous life of sitcoms and deli sandwiches and watching sports . . ."

"But it's cold in Ohio," Fran said. "And I like deli sandwiches." Gretchen laughed. With the potential end of their friendship finally so near, both girls felt a giddiness, and then a clinginess, but they could stay in touch, they reassured each other, if they wanted to, they thought.

Paulina sat in the desk chair in Harvey's office, looking over the figures. "This is how much you'll give me just for the ingredients?" The number made her tingle. She acted bored by it. The week before, she had demonstrated her products on Harvey's sister-in-law in her Upper West Side apartment. Then, a few days ago, Paulina and Harvey had met with a hair scientist who confirmed its effect.

Recently, Paulina had been sleeping in the cramped apartment of a chubby drum teacher named Devon. She cooked dinner and cleaned for him while he gave lessons. At first this arrangement worked fine, but after Paulina failed to attend a band practice of Devon's, he acted coldly toward her. His roommate started latching the deadbolt. Sometimes Devon wouldn't answer his phone, and then Paulina either slept by his door or went out and found some other lonely soul. Sometimes it took hours.

"For the ingredients and the right to own and manufacture the products," Harvey said. "That is, only if it's approved by the FDA." Over the last week, Paulina had gotten used to Harvey. She liked his suits and his mannerisms. His eyes were always flickering, doing the quick work of his mind. He repeatedly ran his hand over his bald head. Paulina liked his wife, Viv, and their Chelsea apartment, and the world of deals and design, private cars and business meetings.

"But what about me? You need me!" Paulina told him. She was wearing her best clothes. She wagged her finger at him.

"I like you, but I don't *need* you. You know nothing about business. What are you, twenty-three? With a *what* degree? An arts degree?"

Paulina gritted her teeth. His original figure was more than enough. It would set her up for a few years. She could finally rent her own place. She so badly wanted a bathroom of her own. She wanted a refrigerator filled with food. A bed she didn't have to share. But why should Harvey have all the fun? What if the labels were tacky?

"Who's going to be the spokesman for this thing?" Paulina asked. "Some middle-aged man? No offense, Harvey, but only I can represent this company! Don't you know anything about PR? Wouldn't it be great press if a twenty-four-year-old genius started her own company? A woman-owned company for a women's hair product?"

Harvey watched Paulina fiddle with the sculptures that decorated his desk. He pictured her face on the website, her signature on the bottle. "What would you call it?" he asked her.

"SUPERCURL," she said with no hesitation.

That sounded okay to Harvey. Nothing mind-bending, but it sounded sharp. She was making all the right points. Still, he could do it without her. He could use his sister-in-law, Rebecca, as the spokeswoman. She had the same kind of hair. "This number is more than fair," he said. "But I can throw on a few more thousand if you'll feel better about it."

Paulina scowled at him. "Listen. I've done my research. I've been to salons. I've seen the horror work they do to curly hair. You can't comprehend the physical pain and mental suffering! SUPERCURL will be the world's best product line for curly hair!"

She was smart, this one—he had to admit it. She'd kept him laughing all week, telling him and Viv all sorts of crazy stories at dinner. And her poor mother had gotten into a horrible boating accident. Harvey could see Paulina's vision and see beyond it. They could make curly hair seem like a cult. Hell, it *was* a cult. Even Rebecca and Paulina, who had little in common, had quickly bonded over their curls.

"SUPERCURL," he said to himself. The phone rang.

"That's right," Paulina said, spinning side to side in her desk chair.

Harvey turned and took the call.

Paulina listened to him talk to someone about something. When he laughed, she worried that it might be at her. She stood as if to leave, to get his eyes back on her, to show him he needed her, but he motioned for her to stay and she sat back down.

Marveling at the cows in the fields, the roadkill on the highway, the schizophrenic voice of the radio, Fran drove her rental car to a small town outside of Cleveland where she had already paid first, last, and security for her new apartment. She flirted with the high school boys who worked the supermarket registers. She befriended stray cats. She took long breaths that meant: *My new life, I am ready, begin!*

It isn't half bad, she wrote in a letter Gretchen took weeks to answer. *There's a record shop and a crêpe place and a park where local bands play in a gazebo.* Fran moved into a basement apartment in an all-studio building. There was always a tenant smoking dejectedly under the awning, even when it was raining, especially when it was raining.

On Fran's first day, Meryl, the woman who interviewed her, led Fran through the Levrett-Mercer office, introducing her. Meryl's tanned skin was loose on her bones. She wore long skirts that failed to conceal her white tennis shoes. Her plainness, her frumpishness, seemed to certify that she was good at math and work.

Meryl pointed to a girl with short red hair. "This is Jane. She's been here for two years. An artist like you." Jane smiled. She had sunken eyes and thin lips. Besides this, she wasn't bad looking. She was even pretty, Fran thought. But Fran found herself focusing on the sunken eyes and thin lips, as if it were a competition to be the prettiest girl in the expansive corporate building.

"I went to MICA," Jane said. Her gray dress pants fit well on her long legs, and Fran saw the outline of small breasts through her white button-down shirt.

"I went to art school too," Fran said, feeling satisfaction from having gone to a better school. Jane smiled, then turned back to her work. Meryl nodded.

"You'll be a floater, like Jane. So every day just come to me when you get here, and we'll find you a spot."

Floaters rotated around the abandoned cubicles. Sometimes one would be referred to as Fred's old cubicle, or Roy's, and Fran would wonder, *What happened to Fred?* And she would imagine a tragic end. The cubicles were nearly identical. Each had a faux wood desk, a boxy black monitor, an adjustable desk chair, a file cabinet, and a company calendar that shrunk the whole year to a few inches.

Fran slouched in an ergonomic chair. She was to write multiple-choice questions for a test to certify high school art teachers. Some of the questions referred to specific pieces of art. Fran could write, "In this painting by Paul Klee, the composition creates which of the following effects?" Then she would write the correct answer, along with three equally plausible answers. The answers had to be similar in sentence construction and length. The format had strict guidelines. Some words could never be used. Only certain artists were eligible. The rules didn't bother Fran—they freed her. She felt glee whenever Meryl approved a new question she'd written. Everyone else used a computer, but Fran wrote on a yellow legal pad. She started wearing panty hose and heels. Her days filled with small problems and small solutions.

The trademark SUPERCURL was registered, and the company founded, in a single week. Paulina was named founder/spokeswoman and Harvey signed her to a generous contract based on projected profits. SUPERCURL filed for patents on Paulina's homemade concoctions for conditioner, styling gel, and frizz guard. There were designers to hire and chemists to consult. After preliminary testing and approval by the FDA, SUPERCURL started outsourcing production. The SUPERCURL conditioner wasn't as strong as Paulina's original recipe. Dyes made it white instead of its usual brown. Fragrances disguised the potent smell.

With Harvey's connections, the company grew quickly. They scouted models, held photo shoots, and signed advertising contracts. High sales in England gave Harvey's investor friends confidence. Some people dismissed Paulina, as if she were the SUPERCURL mascot or even Harvey's daughter, but others seemed to respect her as their colleague. Now she dressed very chic in silk and suede. What she didn't understand, she had her secretary research.

A year later, they worked with an architectural firm to open their flagship salon in SoHo. Paulina knew all the construction workers and tracked their progress daily. She was on the hiring committee and interrogated the stylists and managers. After the salon's grand opening, Paulina was interviewed in *Vogue* in a story titled "Curly World" and photographed with her hair spread out on a pillow. She was quoted saying, "I wish to revitalize the curls of the world." She said the art school had exposed her to "hair in need."

Some days, Harvey regretted his deal with Paulina. Her ideas were good, but she was difficult. She was sensitive. She was always firing her secretary. She told off their head of distribution. Paulina bought things impulsively—an apartment on the Lower East Side, a motorcycle she soon crashed. She bought friends and drugs. She ignored Harvey's advice. Viv started avoiding her at events.

Paulina sat on her love seat wearing a silk kimono. Dinner was over; only the most charred parts of the brussels sprouts were left on the crystal platter, the chicken bones looked grisly piled in a bowl, and the cloth napkins were crumpled on the mirrored table she had imported from India. The straight-backed dining chairs, grandly upholstered in green velvet, were being set back in place by Paulina's maid. Guests sprawled on the oversized leather couch in the living room, noting the excellent condition of Paulina's exposed brick, mesmerized by the chandelier that lorded over them. Candles dripped their wax on silver plates. Music played, but Paulina could not tell who put it on or where it was coming from; everything had been installed while Paulina was on vacation.

Juliette, a young gallery owner Paulina had met at Harvey's one night, bent to scratch the cat. "I can't believe you haven't named him yet!" Paulina stared down at the cat, lean and black, and its companion, fluffy and white. The cats had been a gift from Paulina's stylist for her twenty-fifth birthday. He said if she tired of them, she could just set them loose on the street.

"That one I call Nameless," Paulina said, "and the other is Unknown. But of course I'm open to suggestions."

"What about Cicero?" offered Mimi, Paulina's personal shopper.

"Too grand," said Clive, an ex-boyfriend of Dean's that Dean had sent in his place.

"Dust mite?" said Eli, heir to the Aerobed fortune.

"Jasmine," said Jasmine, a SUPERCURL model Paulina had discovered in the subway. They all laughed. Clive walked over and turned a dial on the wall that appeared to control the music. Paulina watched in wonder. Just the day before, the doorman had told her about Channel 100 on her television, which showed a live feed from the lobby of the building. In black and white, she'd watched her guests arrive to dinner.

Eli and Clive danced lazily and the others threw cushions at them. "Strip!" Paulina ordered, but they refused. Jasmine passed around a carved ivory pipe packed with weed and they smoked. Paulina's throat burned. The smoke added to the good feeling in the room—the sense that there was nowhere else to be. Jasmine told a long story about stealing the pipe from the house of her husband's ex-lover. Paulina gazed at everyone's faces as if they were strangers. The faces moved and Paulina watched them through their quick changes. She heard them talking, but couldn't tell which voice was whose. She'd been pulled from one life and shoved into another. She tried to remember the name of the maid she'd hired.

"Paulina went to Norway too, didn't you?" said Jasmine. Paulina looked up.

"Paulina is in Norway right now," said Eli, and blew smoke in her face.

Paulina laughed. "I went with an old lover of mine. We went discothèque to discothèque." What a wonderful word, "discothèque." How wonderful Fran looked in the discothèque. The white cat walked in and jumped on Paulina's lap. She stroked the creature's soft head.

"What was his name?" Jasmine asked.

"*Her* name." They all laughed and looked at her admiringly, she felt. The old confidence welled in her. "We shacked up with this Nordic god, far away from the world." She felt how their full attention rested on her. "What a time we had there. His castle had a chamber of weapons. He had a trained hawk. We ate bread, and things he had killed, and we drank wine," she said. "He had the most dramatic chest." Paulina pictured Blood Axe like a giant, tall as her windows. "His cock was bigger than Rhode Island. Its arch was designed by Romans. His balls were like two factories populating the world." Her audience smirked at her. "His hair was okay, but the girl had the finest curls I'd seen, beyond my own."

"Where is she now?" asked Clive.

"She's still there." The cat jumped from her lap and brushed against Jasmine's legs. "She chose him over me."

"How could she?" Clive teased, but Paulina took him seriously.

"He was a tremendous lover. His hands. The textures." She shuddered. "He was a terrible filmmaker. But he knew what to do with a woman's body. I could have given her the same, given her better, but still she went with him. She left me." Paulina sighed, reaching for one of the cats, but neither was near.

"What really makes a good lover, do you think?" asked Clive, and everyone answered at once, cutting Paulina's story short. She sat silently through their foolish comments, their boring anecdotes. Their conversation cheapened sex until it seemed the idiot fun of pedestrians and nobodies. Why hadn't Dean showed? Why had he sent his second-rate gay instead, this ex-lover who clearly wanted to join SUPERCURL's marketing team? All during dinner he spoke of his skills, his eye, but Paulina would never hire him. She wasn't allowed to hire people anyway, as Harvey kept reminding her.

Paulina watched Eli play with the cats in a way that would only encourage violence. She turned on Channel 100, looking for interesting people in the lobby. There were none, just the doorman reading the newspaper. She desperately wanted to escape to the balcony, but when Jasmine suggested the balcony and they all cheered, Paulina told them to go without her.

She lay on her back, staring into the chandelier, wondering where Fran was, hoping it was a dark, damp, wretched space, like a war trench or sewer. I hope she's painting faces as a birthday clown in Nebraska, or somewhere that's nowhere, Paulina thought. She wanted Fran to suffer. For even in Paulina's new place, with all of her dreams in reach, the gold letters of her name pressed into her business cards, the intoxicating enthusiasm of her agent, there was still that bundle of misery that traveled along with her, that let out little mites of suffering, even while Paulina laughed, even while she gleamed.

13

Every workday, Fran went to the bathroom about three or four more times than necessary, and hid in the stall listening to the other women, learning how to reload the toilet paper dispenser based on the directions drawn out on the side. Fran no longer felt inspired creating questions. She ruined her eyes looking at tiny JPEGs of masterpieces. She got lightheaded reading about improper ventilation. These things were familiar to her, and yet she was on the other side now, with the nonartists. When she was assigned to work in Denise's old cubicle or Roy's, their departure no longer seemed bleak. They had escaped! They were free! It was *she* who was trapped.

Every now and then, she'd turn a corner in the hallway, suddenly face-to-face with a youngish guy. Their dull faces pulled into quick smiles, and he seemed to feel as Fran did, a look in the eyes. But then it was over and they walked past each other—Fran to the copier like a zombie, the boy to a wing Fran had never seen. Sex seemed the antidote to Levrett-Mercer, or joy and nature and soul music.

Soon there were SUPERCURL salons in LA, San Francisco, San Diego, Seattle, Austin, San Antonio, Chicago, Baltimore, Boston, and Philadelphia. SUPERCURL products were sold in the hippest boutiques. SUPERCURL produced a revitalization treatment, and a CURLS FOR KIDS shampoo. The marketing team created promotions, photo contests, a Curl Club with rules and rewards. The production team designed an Advanced SUPERCURL Hairbrush and Detangler Comb.

Each development was momentous, but Paulina grew used to it. She was still looking for good people to sleep with. For a month she was obsessed with an ego-crazy plastic surgeon she met at a party, but by the end of their short time together she hated him with all her heart. When she walked down the street, the curls of strangers seemed to shine brighter in the sunlight, and she felt a mix of pride and jealousy.

"I definitely notice a difference," Luca told her. Paulina lay facedown on the massage table in her beauty room. Luca was a large, presumptuous Romanian man who dressed in black and called himself the Curly King. He worked exclusively on Paulina's hair, and he also served as her masseuse, her dealer, and sometimes her lover. Luca slept with women and men and lived in a massive basement he called the Dungeon. He often seduced people, then, like picking a lock, drew out their darkest secret before sending them on their way.

Luca stayed inside much of the summer, never wearing shorts, cursing the heat. He hadn't taken a subway since he was a teenager, finding the lighting untenable. He was constantly rewriting his will, deciding who deserved what trifle, ashtray, or mirror. Most of all, he understood hair. He could predict it, and ultimately, control it. One day, he and Paulina planned to merge their curl philosophies and start their own school, The Curl Institute, where hairdressers would study to become SUPERCURL-certified.

"Five, ten years ago, those same girls had bird nests. Frizz balls. You've really cleaned things up," Luca said while he massaged her neck. Paulina knew this to be true, but most days it did not awe her.

"I was once like a peacock, decked out in all magnificence," Paulina told Luca, her face buried in a pillow. "I imagined myself the center of a movement. A political movement, or an art movement, something that combined the two." Paulina still had pizzazz, but the pizzazz had withered. It lay dormant inside her, slipping out in quick, cutting remarks. Luca kept kneading her flesh until the massage became esoteric and neither understood it.

Paulina summoned Fran in her mind. Fran was in a dim place, struggling under a heap of books. "Libraries!" Paulina

cried to Luca. "What a trap for youth!" People didn't think re-
alistically in libraries. People filled their heads with moldy ideas
and left their sexuality in a coil near the stacks, where it turned
to nothing and joined the dust on the floor, swept by losers.

"Huh?" The massage paused while Luca lit a cigarette,
and then reluctantly continued.

"I was just remembering someone."

"Who?" Luca asked.

Paulina considered telling him the whole thing—the art
school, the hotel rooms, the party—but quickly rid herself of
this desire.

"Just this weird farm girl who's probably breeding dogs
somewhere and feeling sorry for herself." Paulina stared into
the wallpaper. "She was cute, like a muffin. Paper skirt and
all. One time she took up with a discarded lover of mine and I
couldn't sleep well until I had him back, to remind myself why
I'd gotten rid of him in the first place. I can't even remember
his name," Paulina said, but it rang in her head like a bell. She
rose from the table and wrapped a sheet around herself.

"Where are you going?" Luca asked.

"Checking the weather," she said and opened her laptop
and typed Julian's name.

That week, Fran was assigned to a highly decorated cube. A
glass jar filled with candy bars sat on a doily. An archaic, sun-

damaged "Got milk?" ad was pinned to the soft cubicle wall. But most distracting was an ultrasound taped above the monitor. Fran stared emotionlessly at the ambiguous shape.

Jane poked her head over the divider. "I think that's the arm," Jane said, pointing.

"No, that's a shadow," Fran said.

"What's the light source?" Jane asked, raising her eyebrows.

"Congratulations nonetheless!" one of the history guys teased.

Jane giggled. "Imagine you with a baby!"

Fran laughed. "Wait, why not?"

"You can't even handle a day's work. Imagine raising a living being? A project you can't leave for me and Meryl to finish," Jane said, nudging her.

Fran and Jane were perpetually on the edge of becoming friends. Every workday they'd share a few jokes, or bond over some obscure nonevent in their office: was Meryl eating an Amy's frozen burrito *again?* Jane would spot the man they'd nicknamed Old Drawers, looking lost in the lobby. Together they'd uncover hilarious outsider art deep in the image bank.

But when Jane invited Fran out on the weekends, Fran never made it. Often she declined immediately with a lie— she had friends coming in that weekend, or she was dogsitting in Columbus. Other times she'd say, "Yeah, sounds good!

I wanna meet your friends for sure." As the appointed time grew closer, though, Fran was inevitably seized with doubt. What if Jane's friends were boring? What if it was awkward? Instead she'd take a nap, then wake up at midnight and walk to a bar covered in flags of the world and talk to guys who gave her their business cards.

Jane nudged her again. "Hey, I wanna check out your studio sometime. You could visit mine too."

"Definitely," Fran said, blushing.

"Mine is near the Institute downtown," Jane said.

"Cool," Fran said. "Mine is a ways out, but I'll draw you a map sometime." She needed to find a studio. Why had it taken her this long? That was the whole point of taking a job in Ohio—finding a nice warehouse space where all the artists hung out dancing, where some hot guy was always welding and NYC gallery owners wandered in off the street. Fran still felt a connection to that world. The other day she'd bought an *Artforum*, hoping to find Paulina's byline on a few reviews. Paulina had once mentioned wanting to write for them.

"Oh, wait, is it in the Art House Studio?" Jane asked.

"No," Fran said, "though I looked at one there."

"The Seventy-Eighth Street Studios?"

"No." Fran nervously twirled a frizzy curl trying to guide it back into shape.

"Where is it? In Shaker Heights?"

"Yeah," Fran said finally. "Close to there." Why did Jane even care?! "I need to make some copies," Fran said, grabbing a handful of papers and walking confidently down the hall.

Suddenly, the young guy was walking toward her. Fran smiled at him. He nodded at her. When he was just about to pass, Fran blurted out, "I have this feeling, like, that we're in *1984*, and we have to escape."

"The year?" he asked.

Fran laughed into her hand. "No, the book. I mean, the civilization in the book. The weird, controlling, conformist society."

"That's weird," he said. They looked each other over. He adjusted and readjusted his watch, then shoved his hands in his pockets. He wasn't any cuter than the guys Fran met at the bars, but she sensed an intelligence within him. She tried to imagine herself passionately kissing his neck, grasping at his chest and arms. Figuring out what he liked sexually. What his silences meant. Where his mind took him when it took him away from her. He shifted uncomfortably. "Haven't read that one in a while. Don't really remember it. Sorry," he said, walking past her, but he didn't sound sorry at all.

Julian's voice was epic in Fran's phone, as if it were coming in from the afterlife. "How did you even find this number?" she asked, amazed. "It's an unlisted landline!"

"It wasn't easy. But once I found out you were working for Levrett-Mercer, I knew I could figure it out. The tutoring company I work for is owned by them."

Fran asked how he was and he told her he'd gone on a terrible vacation to a random place he'd pointed to on a map, and how the locals had sensed this. She asked about his films and he told her he'd sent them to a few dozen festivals but heard nothing back. He'd spent some hours working on a stop-motion animation, but after his hard drive broke he couldn't bear to start over.

"What do you do out there?" Julian asked.

"Boring, boring things," Fran said and he laughed.

"What are you doing tonight?" he asked.

"I was going to go meet up with Jane from work, but now I don't know."

"Now you're just going to stay in and talk to me all night?"

Fran laughed. "Yeah. I wanna hear all about . . . about wherever you live."

"Pittsburgh."

Fran stretched out in her bed and closed her eyes. It was the most relaxed she'd felt in weeks. Julian remembered her. He missed her. He hadn't run out and married someone. He was floundering as badly as she was. "Yeah, tell me all about Pittsburgh." And she actually wanted to know about it. Fran pictured Pittsburgh as windy, with big rusted bridges. For some reason she pictured the people there wearing pilgrim hats, though she knew that was stupid. The name Pittsburgh seemed dignified to her, a place of hanging wooden signs and barbershops, like in old Westerns. A place with no chain stores. Did people trade goods in Pittsburgh? Did they know how to fix cars?

Julian cleared his throat and her heart beat happily in anticipation. She felt like he was offering her a way out, but she didn't have to leave her room.

"What are you wearing?" he asked.

"A purple fleece . . ." she answered.

Paulina sat reading a romance novel on the train to Pittsburgh. The language bored her, yet turned her like a screw in her seat. She ate a floppy, disappointing personal pizza. She thought back to her time in the cold college town, chasing the Color Club boys with Sadie and Allison. She remembered how she and Fran had been new friends once, talking about religion and their bodies, expecting to reach something the other would disagree with, but finding no end. Befriending Fran had been like finding a jewel—a girl whose powerful naiveté was wholly her own.

Julian met her at the Pittsburgh train station. Paulina still found him attractive, though slight wrinkles had formed around his eyes and mouth. He slouched in his wool coat as if resigned to whatever fate was chosen for him. February's hateful winds greeted them outside the station, sweeping Julian's longish hair across his forehead. He looks like a morose Beatle, Paulina thought, pressing her body to his.

Julian's apartment was charmless. Paulina lay in his bed, marveling at the lack. "I would paint this gray wall beige, maybe add a chair rail to the wall, wallpaper the top half in a subtle floral pattern or light geometric. Crown molding up top, and a decent baseboard. The floor could be sanded down to a more spectacular level of grain, and then restained." The room was lit by an overhead fixture that belonged in a dorm room or cell.

Then they were having sex and Paulina found it difficult to kiss him. She tried to at first—he was so eager for everything—but ultimately she turned her head away and kissed his arm instead. After, they lay in the dark. Julian's hands brushed again and again against her breasts in a way that would usually have annoyed her, but tonight soothed her. Paulina thought of Fran, her legs and her laugh, the way she twirled her hair while distracted.

"Remember Thai Dream?" Julian said. Paulina's heart sank.

"No," she said, and he laughed.

Paulina remembered one night when she and Fran took the wrong Metro in Norway. Instead of the downtown, they saw rows and rows of houses with red-tiled roofs. For a moment it all felt hopeless—they were exhausted and had a long day of museums and lectures the next day—but then Fran ran a few steps and clicked her heels like they were in a paradise. A boisterous group of Norwegian teens passed, wearing bell-bottoms and puffy winter jackets, and Paulina started walking with them to make Fran laugh. Paulina kept pace with the group and Fran followed too, for blocks and blocks, until they arrived at a nearby house party.

At the party, Paulina and Fran had talked only to each other. They danced with the teens in someone's bedroom, at one point chasing each other through the kitchen and the living room, where an old man was watching television and breathing through a ventilator.

The Metro was no longer running when they returned late that night, but Paulina was able to find a cab, and even convinced the driver that she was an American pop star. Paulina remembered Fran smiling with her eyes closed, her head on Paulina's lap, while Paulina played with her hair. Paulina had insisted on paying for the cab, though it was nearly the last of her kroner. Later, she'd had to steal some from Marissa to get by, but it had been worth it to walk arm in arm into the hotel, where, if she remembered right, a sleepy concierge had winked at them and offered them macaroons.

The memory left Paulina with such a strong sense of Fran

that she imagined it was Fran who was now getting out of bed and walking off toward the bathroom. That night in Norway, she remembered Fran pulling her nightgown down over her breasts. What had Paulina said then? Hadn't she said something funny? Or had she just stared?

Paulina rose from the bed and followed the phantom into the bathroom. Stray pubic hairs were visible on the checkerboard floor. An insistent drip had worn away the porcelain sink, leaving a rust stain. Julian's body in the act of peeing disgusted her. Paulina found herself examining his gray toothbrush, the worn bristles sticking in all directions. Her legs were now completely absent of magic. The toothbrush displeased her. A crusty accumulation of paste sat low in its bristles. She threw it in the garbage can.

"What's the meaning?" said Julian, his penis soft, his balls slack.

"I'm giving you mine," Paulina said, pointing to the new one she had brought. Julian snickered at her, then brushed his teeth in an exaggerated manner.

14

At school, Julian had resented how much time and energy Paulina and Fran stole from him. They sought him out in the editing room. They kept him from his work. And when they stayed away, he compulsively summoned them back—mentally replaying their latest dramas, desiring one, then suddenly the other. During crits, he'd said little to help the flawed films of his classmates and had made no lasting friendships.

After school, he'd moved into his dead uncle's apartment and spent his summer days walking the streets of Pittsburgh. Past the dim-colored houses, the garages built into hills, he smiled at the McBubbles Car Wash sign, the Heinz sign. He peered into abandoned Blockbusters, was heckled by a homeless man who called him Slim. He glared at the Carnegie Mellon kids in Warhol T-shirts, jealous of the anticipation on their bright faces.

He met Internet dates at crumb-covered coffee shops—

dental hygienists who didn't take his ambitions seriously, starry-eyed college students who talked over him, sequins flashing that they'd *rather be dancing*. Drunken dates used him as a sounding board, recounting their bad childhoods and newfound allergies. Perhaps most frustrating were the bookish girls who messaged back and forth with him about novels and movies, never responding to his invitation to meet, satisfied to write letters until their deaths.

Eventually he'd fallen in love with Michelle, one of his married students, a musician and composer hoping one day to get a PhD. Michelle had more grace than Paulina and Fran combined. She was smarter than him, she was sensible, but her husband limited every aspect of their time together. Julian saw him in framed photographs in their house and once at the butcher's counter at the store, buying more frozen shrimp than one person could eat.

Guilt aside, the affair revived him. He started writing movies and taking walks again. He read books with drawings of flowers on their covers, helplessly psychedelic, or tired, limp pen-and-ink drawings of Japanese fish. He cooked for Michelle and took her on weekend trips when her husband was away on business. Julian fantasized the husband's death or mysterious disappearance, but the man kept returning unscathed.

When the affair ended and Michelle no longer responded

to his texts or e-mails, Julian fell into the same lovesick dread he'd felt at school. Unshowered and brooding, he watched all the Bond movies sequentially, unable to make himself do laundry or go to the supermarket. He joined Facebook, waiting for Fran to appear, but she had never liked the Internet, had never understood how it worked. He remembered how she'd researched her art history papers in the library, instead of using Google the way he'd shown her.

Julian spent his days on the Internet, reading all the different kinds of news, tracking the weather he watched through his window. He watched graphic videos of assassinations, illegally downloaded programs he didn't need and didn't use. He lingered in the comments sections, where the conversation always turned irrelevant and ugly. The Internet misled him. It took him so many places he forgot to leave his desk.

Julian and Fran spent hours on the phone, having long, convoluted heart-to-hearts. One Friday, after work, Fran finally went to the train station and bought a ticket to Pittsburgh. Julian had offered to come visit her many times, but she was embarrassed by her small town and the eccentric neighbors she'd unconsciously befriended. How could she explain that she and Violet did *puzzles* together and drank hot chocolate? Her Ohio apartment was just normal. It wasn't painted the bright colors of the art school. It had no funny shrines to Johnny Cash, no florescent rock installations in the bathroom.

On the train, Fran recalled young Julian seducing her. He'd been a thin dream of someone's. She remembered the frazzled hairs pointing away from his erection, his intense stare. She started drafting a letter to Gretchen in her head. *You won't believe this, but I'm about to see Julian after so many years! And he's single, he says. And I'm definitely single. And I brought condoms . . .*

When she got to Pittsburgh she walked languidly around the station, half-smiling in case he was watching from across the room. She wanted to see him before he saw her, but he was nowhere.

At the line of sinks in the bathroom, she wet a curl of hers that had separated. She listened to two girls laughing and smoking in one of the stalls. *I think he stood me up, Gretchen. Isn't this absurd?* All the sinks had automatic faucets, but one was running even though no one was near it. Fran tried to fix it, waving her hands under its stream, but the faucet would not turn off. She let it run. With nothing else to do, she examined her face in the mirror, pleased with the face that looked back at her, though she tried to keep this satisfaction from the strangers walking past.

When she left the bathroom, Julian was there. He gave her a big hug. Fran pressed her face hard into his coat. "I'm sorry I'm late," he said. "I would have texted you, but you're the only person on earth without a cell phone." She demurred proudly. "I borrowed my neighbor Joel's car to pick you up." He took her hand and they walked to the parking lot, feeling young and watched.

Julian wanted to kiss Fran when they got in the car, but she was looking wistfully into the distance and he didn't want to rush things. "Are you into this?" he asked, starting the engine.

"What?"

"This. Me. Pittsburgh. Joel's Volvo. The weather."

"I'm into it," Fran said. "I feel good." She leaned over and kissed him.

Julian led her up the three flights to his apartment. Fran gave him the old, good feeling. He wouldn't push her away this time. Fran could get him over Michelle, the way Michelle had gotten him over Fran, the way Fran had gotten him over Paulina. He looked at Fran's profile approvingly. Looking at her, he could remember them splayed on his bed that one summer, stiffly going to their first fancy restaurant, filming her in the bathtub with his Bolex.

They walked into his apartment and Fran set down her bag. "Do you have a mirror?" she asked Julian, touching her hair. Already her hair felt different than it had at the station. Every day it seemed to get dryer.

"There's a small one in the bathroom," he said. She wandered toward it. His apartment was like hers, absent of joy. A lonely painting hung unevenly off the wall, its thrift store price tag still glued on. To look in his dusty bathroom mirror was to see oneself through a stranger's eyes.

The sex was as good as it had been, was made better by her sexless time in Ohio. Julian gave her his love back. He treated each part of her body like a precious thing that told the story of mankind, even her elbows and earlobes. He listened intently as she reluctantly told him about the Bushwick loft, Gretchen's success, the test questions she lay awake creating in Ohio.

Fran felt her old personality whirling around her. She teased him about the copy of *Mein Kampf* in his bookcase. "Is that to scare away your one-night stands? You should have a whole shelf like that. A shelf of horror." Julian laughed.

"I do! I have some medical textbooks," he squinted across the room.

"*A History of Cannibalism*," she said. Every time he laughed she felt relief. She'd found a loose thread from her past and could follow it back to herself.

The next morning, sunlight danced on Fran's face. Julian reached for her and held her. His radio started playing music. Fran looked at a spider's web that stretched between Julian's dresser and the wall. The spider was alive like her. Some life energy connected her to it and to everything. *The future was going to be easy!* Fran thought, rummaging through her bag for underwear. *She didn't need to meet a new person! She didn't need to change!*

She saw it on the floor while getting dressed. "It's hers," Fran said. The hair clip looked tiny on the floor, but she recognized it. Suddenly, Fran recalled Paulina's voice, her unnerving cackle, the foreign elegance she lent a place.

Julian sat up in his bed. "She's visited once or twice. She called me last month and it got me thinking of you again." He tried to gauge if she was jealous. Jealousy was a good sign.

Fran stared at the hair clip, letting her eyes blur and focus on it. "Once or twice?" she asked him.

"Twice," he said.

"Fuck," Fran said. "I feel crazy."

Why couldn't he just pick one of them? *Fucking flip a coin*, she thought. And why did Paulina still want him? Just to torture her? Fran's head throbbed. And now she was going to cry in front of Julian, who was never moved by tears.

"Come back to bed, babe."

Fran bent down and picked it up.

"What are you going to do, smell it?" Julian asked.

Fran cursed him off. The hair clip was the same kind Paulina had used in college; it might even have been one she'd worn back then. Fran put the hair clip in her hair. It made a satisfying click.

"That's it," Julian said, relaxing. "It's yours. This is all yours. I don't need to see her anymore." This was true. He felt it like a candle lighting his being. When Joel had asked about Paulina, Julian had described her as "a benevolent monster who fucks well." Of course she was funny too, and smart, and had bought him a huge steak at the fanciest restaurant in Pittsburgh. He loved her, but she diminished in his memory.

"Really, I just want you," he said.

"Yeah?" Fran crawled onto his bed and Julian pulled the covers around her. He kissed her face and her neck and her hair and her shoulders.

"Yeah," he said, pulling her shirt back off. They started kissing again, and grabbing each other. Julian got on top of her. Fran imagined Paulina in quick muddled flashes, each vision bringing her closer to orgasm.

"I don't care if you see her again," Fran said, naked against Julian. "But it is a little nostalgic of her."

"And it's not of you?" Julian turned off the lamp, filling the room with a bluish doom.

"She's the one who's so against nostalgia."

Julian shrugged. "She started this hair product business," he said. Fran laughed. "You haven't heard about it?" Julian

asked. "SUPERCURL. It's all over the place. They're even building a salon in Pittsburgh." Fran had seen ads for the product,
but she'd had no idea it was Paulina's. She acted unimpressed,
but her jealousy spread like a rash.

"I really wish I could paint again," said Fran, instantly
regretting it. This statement inevitably lead to the tired discussion of fumes vs. studio costs, oil vs. acrylic, lukewarm
suggestions involving watercolor or Photoshop. It reminded
her of a visual arts test question.

"Just use acrylic," Julian said. "Who's stopping you?"

Acrylic paint was uninspiring; it lacked that oily, sexy
smell. Fran kissed him to shut him up. They heard a hacking
cough through the wall.

"What's that?" she asked.

"Alma," he said.

"That doesn't sound good," Fran said.

"No, it can't be good."

The next morning Julian made her pancakes, and it was still
fun. They hadn't run out of jokes. Still, Fran told herself she
was never coming back. It felt good and eerie to be near him,
but she didn't need him. While he was going to the bathroom,
she took Paulina's old student card, which she'd all these years
kept in her wallet, and left it facedown next to a dead cactus
on his table.

. . .

At Jane's opening, Fran was startled to see that Jane was very talented. Her paintings were intricate Bosch-like scenes of caves and valleys crowded with people from different time periods looking at their cell phones, pointing guns, skinning animals, proposing to each other. The figures were just an inch or two, Fran estimated, but each one had a personality painted in.

The gallery filled with people. Good music was playing. There was a spread of food on a long table. Everyone was excited by the paintings. They seemed like something Fran had imagined, had meant to paint herself. Something she would eventually have stumbled upon.

Fran wondered if Paulina was with Julian this weekend and knew she was.

"Fran!" Jane called, and walked over holding the hand of a tall, slender blond. "This is Deena," Jane said, squeezing the girl's hand. The girl wore a low-cut black dress. Her hair was shiny and straight. It glistened under the lights.

"Great to meet you," Deena said. Fran stared at them. Was it possible they were *together*? They couldn't be. Fran would have heard about it. Fran would have been able to sense a vibe from Jane, a gay vibe. Fran got lost looking at Deena's lips. Deena had dark green eyes and lines on her eyelids where her mascara had smudged. As Fran watched Jane and Deena talk

and laugh, it seemed so natural, something she and Paulina
could have been, long ago in the college town, without Julian,
or Marvin, or any jerk with nice eyes. "Are you a painter
too?" Deena asked.

"Oh, no, I'm Jane's coworker," Fran said haltingly. Jane
and Deena laughed as if Fran had said something hysterical.
They were drunk on love. Fran looked at the paintings, wanting to own them. She laughed too, wanting to be a part of
whatever was between Jane and Deena, whatever elusive luck
they'd mined together, whatever delivered their happiness to
them.

That night, Fran took out her cracked watercolors, her stiff
acrylics, her congealed oils. She painted on the cardboard box
her desk chair came in. She painted cartoonish blobs, naked
women, crossed-out faces, burning cities, hairlike forms she
turned into clouds, dogs wearing clothes. Everything she
painted looked very much like her work before art school, like
the doodles she'd drawn in high school, that she still drew
during Levrett-Mercer meetings.

The red boots were by the door when Fran walked into Julian's. "She left them for you," Julian said, as if they were all
roommates. Paulina had worn the boots at Eileen's thing;
Fran had complimented her on them. In Norway, Paulina had

looked for boots like these, finding nothing like them. Fran tried them on. They were too big and didn't match her outfit, but she wore them all weekend.

Fran asked so many questions about Paulina that Julian finally said, "Why don't you just call her? I can give you her number."

"No, no, that's okay," Fran said. "We'd have nothing to say to each other." She was careful not to say anything more about Paulina for the rest of the weekend. But she found herself looking at each object in Julian's house—the ladybug caught between windows, the big crystal paperweight, the dirty inside of the microwave—wondering what Paulina thought about it. In the bathroom, Fran looked at herself in the dusty mirror and wondered what Paulina would think of her. With her finger she wrote "Hi" in the dust.

"I don't understand," Paulina said, toying with her new dress. Harvey paced in front of his office window. Paulina watched the sharp lines of his suit as he pulled his phone from his pocket, glanced at it, then slid it back.

"With the rise of Luxene, we've been considering offers we haven't considered before." Luxene was Johnson and Johnson's new curl line. The women in marketing were stressed about it, but Paulina wasn't afraid of competition. Harvey yanked up his venetian blinds, revealing a sunset over New Jersey. "You don't go to the meetings, so it's hard to catch you up."

"I've been busy," Paulina said, picking up a stray hair and letting it fall on the floor. "Are you seriously considering selling?" she asked as her phone vibrated in her hand. "Because that would be ridiculous," Paulina said, peeking at Luca's text.

"I'm trying to be reasonable with you, but after much consideration—"

"I refuse to step down and I won't be bought out."

Harvey sighed. "The incident," he began. Harvey's secretary appeared momentarily in the door's window, but Harvey waved her off. Paulina sweated in her new dress. Weeks ago, at a benefit for something or other, when an attractive man asked if she would donate to the charity he managed, she agreed immediately. She was just going to give money, but then thought of how hair products could improve the lives of the homeless. The next day she put in a bulk order for them. It was all good-natured, she told herself again. Her actions had been grossly misunderstood. The charity leaked the details to a newspaper. Harvey and everyone had gotten so moralistic on her. What had they ever done for the homeless?!

"Can't you ever get past that?" Paulina asked with much restraint, her phone buzzing again.

Harvey wore his anger neatly. "You fucked up. You went

over my head. You didn't talk to Garrett like you're supposed to. It caused a lot of bad press."

Paulina had heard this speech many times before, but this time she didn't interrupt him. Usually when he scolded her, she fantasized about murdering him, poisoning him, drowning him, establishing her alibi, but this time she forced herself to listen to him, to look at him plainly, as if there weren't a war inside her.

"*Vogue* pulled our ads. *Hair Monthly* postponed our article. Sometimes you hurt this company more than you realize."

Paulina tried to channel her hatred and fear into something more effective. She smoothed her hair back and gave Harvey a smile. *Remember that time Garrett left his browser tabs up on his laptop?* she wanted to say, but now that felt like so long ago. She'd barely seen Harvey in the past few months. He had some overseas Botox deal he was developing. He hadn't invited her anywhere in a long time. She was no longer listening to what he was saying. She found herself longing for Fran again, but couldn't bear to ask Julian for her number.

"Some people think it might be easier if you were less involved."

Paulina tried to comprehend this. She took a breath and zoomed out, saw them momentarily like two dolls in a play office. But it was ludicrous! She'd been doing a good deed!

"I refuse to step down and I won't be bought out."

"Your contract has a clause in it to cover situations like this. It might simplify things. You'd get paid plenty you know." Harvey sat in his chair again. He had her, and he'd finally managed to tell her without being interrupted.

Paulina was speechless. She would lock him in a tomb! Take him on a long drive and then leave him on the highway. She wanted to tie him to a tree and then shoot arrows at him. She could take him to court! She would sway the jury. Or maybe just trash his office. Wreck his car. At the very least, delete him from her phone—the phone SUPERCURL bought her. Paulina stared at the puny Newark skyline feeling sentimental.

"I'm truly sorry," she managed, after a long pause. "I acted impulsively, and then some might say defensively. But I feel so much a part of this company, and I'll start going to meetings again, and try to think big picture, and consider whatever deals you're thinking about."

Harvey's adrenaline slowed as Paulina spoke, leaving a queasy feeling in its wake. It was one of her best apologies. He had finally scared some sense into her. Deep down, he liked her. She kept things exciting. But this was his chance to cut free. If he didn't do it, Viv would say, "I told you so." She'd bring it all up again: the Pantene confidentiality leak, the birthday party she'd ruined with her obnoxious date. She'd say that Paulina discriminated against people with straight hair. Suddenly Harvey remembered Paulina's drunken speech at the Milan opening, and almost smiled.

"Well," he mumbled uncertainly. "If you really will co-operate . . ." Something soft and good was rising within him. Viv would kill him when she found out. But he liked this un-expected feeling. It kept telling him how reasonable he was, how totally unlike his father he'd become. How generous, how honorable.

"We could give you a lesser role," Harvey heard himself saying. "You could still keep your office. You would still be one of the founders."

Tears formed, but Paulina willed them back in her eyes. She didn't need any favors! She and Luca would start their Curl Institute. She had so much money. She had so much style! But she couldn't bear to watch SUPERCURL burn on with-out her. She pictured some fool in her office. She could see it now—Harvey's new Wave Line products, already stupid, paving the way for Straight Line products.

"Okay," Paulina said.

Harvey looked defeated. They stared at each other. Harvey waited for Paulina to thank him. Paulina waited for him to apologize.

"Remember that time we saw Garrett's computer," Paulina said, "and he'd written in to that medical site asking about his rash, and in another window he had a cat adoption site open, and a dating site, and some article on how to get gum out of denim?"

Harvey smiled.

"You'll be glad you kept me on," Paulina said. "Really." She wanted him to beam with joy. "Truly," she said, looking hard at his face.

"Good," he said, waving his secretary in. The woman gave Paulina a pitying look, then immediately started talking about Luxene. Paulina listened, keeping her opinions to herself.

"Like a trip?" Fran asked. Julian nodded. All weekend, Fran had looked for signs of Paulina and found none. The mirror had been cleaned, her sad, dusty "Hi" now gone. There were no tampon wrappers in the garbage, no lotions by the sink.

"A romantic getaway," Julian said, pleased.

"What's wrong with here?"

"Nothing. But this will be somewhere new, somewhere neither of us have been. I've heard it's really beautiful." He ran his finger down her arm.

"In Lancaster?" Fran asked.

"Near it. If you take the train here Friday night, we can drive up. I rented a car." She tried to imagine this. Would there be a little shack by the lake? Would she wear a little nightie thing, like she was losing her virginity?

She searched the room again for anything new. The nightstand, the closed blinds, the dresser. She saw that the spider had abandoned his web; the sagging threads were now coated with dust. There was a pile of thick novels by Russian writers, some dollars crumpled on dirty socks, the broken plastic laundry bin. "Whose umbrella is that?" Fran asked. It was elegant, black.

"Joel's. I had to borrow it." Julian touched her cheek. "Kids and all that. Do you still want them?"

"Do you?"

"I could have some kids, if you wanted some. Where did you want to move again? Canada? I could move to Canada," he said. Her old dreams sounded dreary and difficult now. *Canada?* The coughing started up again. There was a sound of a chair pushing against the floor. Fran and Julian looked to the wall, while the coughing continued.

"Should we call a doctor?" Fran asked.

"Is there a doctor in the house?" Julian asked, looking around. Fran laughed and grabbed him.

"What about the movies? Weren't you going to make films?" Fran asked. The coughing spell continued. Julian waited for it to finish, then walked to the bathroom. As she watched him, she thought she saw something on his butt—a tattoo or something. "What is that?"

"What?" he asked.

"Nothing," Fran said. She'd probably imagined it. She

pictured next weekend, in Lancaster, *near* Lancaster. But, no, she'd seen something there, on the back of him. She tried to put it out of her mind while he hummed in the bathroom. She saw herself pregnant with his child, standing near a big picture window, looking out at a yard. She saw her pregnant self near the Canadian window, holding something . . . a cup of tea? She didn't really drink tea. She stared at the wall Julian shared with Alma. Fran had seen her once in the hallway. The old woman was tiny. She probably hadn't started out that size. People shrank, grew inward.

When he was asleep, Fran turned on his book lamp. He slept soundly on his side, his head facing away from her. She gently pulled the sheet down. "Love you," he murmured, then snored at her. She wanted to laugh. She pulled the sheet to his thighs and examined his long torso. On one of his lean butt cheeks, in faint pen, she saw Paulina's handwriting:

215 grand st. apt #11

10 next friday

15

Fran stared at the Post-it where she'd copied down the address. On her work computer, she looked up what subways were near there. What did Paulina want with her anyway? Fran wasn't going to fly all the way to New York just to have Paulina insult her and make her promise never to see Julian again. Paulina was like that. If you took something of hers, it was never forgotten. You were never free.

"Fran, we need more questions about art careers. Jane wrote a few good ones, but we need at least ten for the standard," Meryl said, leaning over the divider of Fran's cube. "There's a bunch of books that might help in the library, but this should help too." She handed Fran an overstuffed folder of printouts and pamphlets.

Fran wouldn't give Paulina the satisfaction. Instead she'd be in Julian's arms somewhere near Lancaster on a *romantic getaway*, which must mean "sex in a new place." In the cube across from her, Ray, who worked in the history department, was bragging to another man about a streak of "hits" he'd had. A hit was a test question that was conceived, written, and accepted for use in one pass.

"I had like twenty hits, my longest streak, in '97," Ray said. "Do you remember that?" The other man murmured. Ray whistled. "You know what? Crazy thing is that was right in the middle of my divorce." The men were silent.

"Hits can be like that," the other man said. "The brain works better in times of upheaval. Men are at their most creative."

Fran rolled her eyes. Levrett-Mercer was filled with the most boring men alive. People who took too much pleasure in being right. "Let's look it up!" they exclaimed at the first sign of disagreement.

Jane poked her head into Fran's cube. "Aren't the career questions weird?"

"How do you mean?" Fran asked. Now that Fran knew Jane liked girls, it seemed obvious. But why didn't Jane like *her*? Fran couldn't help but envy her. Jane went home to her girlfriend every day. Jane went to her *art studio*. She no longer invited Fran to hang out after work, and now Fran wanted to. Fran wanted to see Jane and Deena, what kind of life they made together. Did they have a beautifully designed apartment, with modern furniture and dustless surfaces? Or did they live in a kind of lesbian squalor, with ratty tapestries on the floor, bras by the bed, and weed on the table?

"Just, like, how *this* is a career in the visual arts—writing questions at L-M. It's sort of meta," Jane said.

"Ha. Yeah. I guess I don't think of this as a visual arts career," Fran said. "It's just a job with a visual arts *theme*."

"Well, look through the pamphlet. Let me know if you find something better," Jane said.

"I will!" Fran got excited. Levrett-Mercer was paying her to research a better job! She opened the folder. There were a series of flyers with grim statistics. She flipped through a few photocopied articles. One of them, titled "Before You Choose a Visual Arts Career," was a cautionary tale written by a self-important watercolor artist.

It was someone's birthday in the Math Department, and from across the hall Fran could hear a small crowd of voices going through the dragging birthday song. She found a packet called *Careers in the Visual Arts*. In the back was a list of all the possible art careers.

Advertising Editor

Animator

Architect

Art Auctioneer

Art Critic

Art Historian

Art Restorer

Art Teacher

Art Therapist

Bookbinder

Calligrapher

Candlemaker

Caricature Artist

Ceramist

Costume Designer

Enamelist

Fabric Draper

Florist

Gallery Owner

Gift Wrapper

Glassblower

Graphic Designer

Hair Stylist

House Painter

Illustrator

Industrial Designer

Interior Decorator

Jeweler

Letterer

Makeup Artist

Medical Illustrator

Muralist

Museum Curator

Paperhanger

Parade Float

Photographer

Printmaker

Sculptor

Set Designer

Silversmith

Stained Glass Restorer

Stone Mason

T-shirt Designer

Tattoo Artist

Textiles Designer

Theater Director

Weaver

Window Decorator

Woodworker

Parade Float? What the fuck. How was that an option? It seemed like an insult, a spectacle of failure and self-promotion. Decorating oneself lavishly like a fool, or getting fat and dropping out of society. Also—*gift wrapper?!* That was not an art. Where was *painter?*

"Look at this! It's so fucked up," Fran said, shaking the pamphlet at Jane.

Jane scanned it, amused. "I don't get it. Glassblower, graphic designer. Looks okay to me." Jane handed it back.

"No, here," Fran emphatically circled Parade Float.

Jane cracked up. "That's just a typo. They mean 'parade float designer,'" Jane said. Fran sighed. "What? It's a real thing."

"It feels demoralizing. Everything is hopeless. I'm going to quit today," Fran said. She stared at Jane and imagined she was Jane's lover, lying with her under the covers, going grocery shopping. Whatever Jane and Deena did together—hosting game nights? watching awards shows?—Fran would be good at that. Or, better yet, she could be Deena's lover. Lie in Deena's arms. Brush Deena's long straight hair away from her face.

"Are you sure? You're probably just having a bad day. Tell Meryl you're sick and go home early."

"I'm a painter. Not a writer of test questions. I hate tests. I hate questions." Fran ran her hand through her hair. "Ugh! This job has ruined my hair. It's like straw, touch it."

Jane touched it. "It's not that bad, Fran." Tears waited in Fran's eyes. "You can't quit," Jane said, but Fran was already walking to Meryl's desk. In no time at all, she had quit Levrett-Mercer, signed the forms, and handed in her key card.

Fran stood triumphantly outside Levrett-Mercer in a drizzly rain. She was like a bug who'd been trapped in a window for days, but had finally located the tear in the screen.

"Fran, wait," Jane called, walking out the door without a jacket.

Fran, wait, I love you, Fran thought. *I'm very attracted to you. Me and Deena both. We've been meaning to ask you . . .*

"What will you do for money?" Jane asked.

Fran looked at the bus stop a few yards away, where she'd spend the next thirty minutes waiting on a metal bench. "I'll live with Julian. I'll borrow money from Paulina."

"Who's Julian?" Jane asked.

"My boyfriend," Fran said. "He's taking me to Lancaster this weekend," she said, matter-of-factly.

"Wow! I had no idea you were seeing someone. Since when?"

"Junior year of college."

"Oh my god, Fran! You're practically married," Jane said.

"What? No. It's not like that."

"We should go on a double date. Me and Deena will cook you dinner."

Fran smiled at her. "I would love that. I really liked Deena."

Fran hugged Jane. She liked how Jane smelled. She imagined a perfume called Lesbian Squalor. Maybe that's how Deena smelled. Maybe she'd find out.

The hairdresser touched Fran's hair and recoiled. "I know it's really dry," Fran said. "That's why I came in. Can't you give me a strong conditioner or something?" The salon had that plastic smell of vanity and fear. It was decorated with black-and-white photos of models. Silver blow dryers sat out on the counters like big flamboyant guns. Fran usually cut her own hair.

The hairdresser was a thin European. He furrowed his brow. His accent made Fran feel ordinary. He fluffed her hair with distaste. "Well, I can use these new products we just got in," he said, pointing to a bottle labeled SUPERCURL. The logo was written in scribbly letters above a line drawing of a woman's wild curls. Below her was a drawing of a man who looked exactly like Marvin. Fran examined his sweet, sweet face. They had captured it and now it was everyone's.

Fran stared at the sleek, simple hair of the models in the photos on the wall.

"Can you just straighten it? That's what I want."

"Are you *sure?* We have a chemical called KillKurl, but it's permanent. It's harsh on hair, and yours is already so dry. The SUPERCURL deep conditioner would revitalize it. You've got such beautiful curls—"

"Straighten it."

The hairdresser looked at her with disdain. His own hair was tightly cropped to his head, but he moved with inherent style. "It's a long, intense process. I'd have to apply it, let it sit, do my eleven o'clock, and then rinse it off. It breaks the natural bonds of the hair. It erases your hair's memory."

It smelled like burning. Fran sat under a dryer, her hair bundled and clipped in foil, fighting nature. Looking at the glossy fashion magazines on the table, Fran was stunned to see Paulina on the cover of *Hair Monthly*. Paulina had grown into the sophistication of her face, like it had been her face's great plan all along. Fran ducked under the dryer to reach for the magazine. She found the article and started to read.

Paulina Hermanowitz, 26, is the young entrepreneur behind the curly hair revolution. The past two years have seen SUPERCURL double in revenue and become a salon favorite. SUPERCURL has deviated from industry standards with their new male campaign "Curls aren't just for girls," which has introduced their products to the other half of the population.

Graphic designer Gretchen Peterson designed SUPERCURL's new curlyboy logo.

Things haven't always been easy for the new company. Hermanowitz was widely criticized last fall when she donated SUPERCURL products to the homeless in lieu of a monetary contribution.

Fran didn't want to know any more. Things had wound themselves together too tightly. Fran flipped to the next article, detailing the ways hair changes during pregnancy. She spent a few minutes looking at an illustrated timeline of the history of braiding.

The dryer droned on. It warmed her ears until they stung. Fran could feel the chemical working. It was undoing all the senseless coils. Unconsciously, she started to compose a montage of hair memories—boys in middle school playing with her curls, pulling them and letting them bounce up, strangers stopping her on the street telling her how jealous they were.

Fran felt deserted under the dryer. The salon filled with gaudy suburban moms. The European hairdresser drifted about, teasing everyone, kissing customers good-bye on both cheeks. His eleven o'clock arrived—a teenage girl with thick, unruly curls. The hairdresser applied SUPERCURL Deep Conditioner while the girl's mother looked on, relieved.

Finally the hairdresser raised the dryer's head, took off

the plastic shower cap, and led Fran to the sinks. "Rinse her, Amy," he said, and the water started. The woman's hands caressed Fran's scalp. Fran remembered the time in the bathroom in college, exhausted from dancing. She thought about what train she would take, the J or the 6. Then it was back under the dryer. The hair dryer worked its anger at her. *Don't go to New York*, it said. She had already quit Levrett-Mercer. Quitting Julian would leave her with nothing.

Fran's new hair fell flatly away from her face. Instead of clinging together, it feathered out, escaping her. The hairdresser tried to act enthusiastic, but even he seemed to know that Fran had been condemned. "Give it a few days. The hair needs time to recover from the shock." His phone chirped from his pocket. He pulled it out and glanced at the screen, laughing quietly. He unsnapped the salon gown from Fran's neck, releasing her from his responsibility. He talked cheerfully with the other customers while she fumbled with her wallet. The worst part was, she had to pay him for it. She had to *tip* him!

The next morning, Fran woke up hung over, thinking of Julian. Gradually, she recalled the small details of her life. It was Friday. She didn't have to go to Levrett-Mercer. Fran wanted to rejoice! She got out of bed and started her morning routine. She would take an early train to Pittsburgh. If she got there early enough, she could cab to Julian's and surprise him before he started work around lunchtime. This energized her. She started to throw socks and underwear into the old patchwork backpack. *What was the weather in Lancaster this weekend?* Fran didn't have time to check.

The mirror stilled her. She took Paulina's hair clip from her bureau and pinned back a section of limp hair. It didn't improve it. Fran undid the clip and put it in her pocket. She wanted to scream. She wet her hair in the sink and it hung even straighter. She'd figure out something on the train.

Fran stood in front of the long bathroom mirror in Pittsburgh's Penn Station. On one side of her, a young girl expertly applied lipstick. On the other side, a homeless woman rinsed her mouth. Fran tried ineffectually to twirl her damp hair into curls. The young girl watched with interest, before following her mother's voice away from the sinks. Fran wet her hair down again and combed it out with her fingers.

She looked like an animal that had fallen in a pool. This was not ideal for a romantic getaway. She would have to get a perm somewhere. She had to get a perm now. She wandered through the station, pausing to think under the stunning rotunda, looking for a stranger who would let her use his phone. Strangers walked in every direction, but Fran hesitated, unable to stop them. They passed her silently. Some turned back to look at her, sensing that she wanted something from them. Couples passed hand in hand. Fran would never interrupt a couple. Couples were on their own journeys.

Finally, Fran saw a teenage girl pulling a rolling suitcase. The girl had short spiky hair. Fran approached her smiling. The girl listened reluctantly.

"I'm sick," Fran said to Julian.

"Oh, baby, that's horrible. What's this number you're calling me from?" She could tell she'd awakened him. She pictured how the light hit his bed in long stripes at this time of day.

"It's the doctor's office phone," Fran said. The girl stared at her in disbelief.

"What's wrong?"

"The flu, they think."

"I'm going to come out there and take care of you."

"No, no," Fran said quickly. "Let's just see each other next weekend. I'll rest up for it." The girl gave her a resentful look. Fran turned away from her.

"I have to wait a whole week?" He sounded forlorn.

"I'm really sorry. Maybe I'll get there a day early."

"What about work?" Julian asked. The girl sighed impatiently.

"I'll take a sick day. I'm taking one right now."

"Sounds like a plan, Fran," he said with labored cheer.

"Can you get a refund on the room and the car?"

Fran pictured a cool, relaxing lake, a little white house with blue shutters, and a garden with gray, weather-damaged statues. Next to it sat an old rented Buick covered in sunlight. Her mind even conjured up a good-natured mutt, running toward her through the grass.

"Don't worry about me. Just take care of yourself," he said. Fran felt a burst of love for him.

"I love you." The girl put her hand out for the phone.

"I love you too," Julian said, only a few miles away.

Fran handed the phone back to the girl. The girl studied her, as if deciding her age, or where she came from, or what would become of her.

"It's not usually like this," Fran said. "My hair, I mean. It's usually curly."

"Whatever," the girl said and quickly wheeled her luggage away.

Fran would go back to Ohio. A train to New York would cost $150 and take nine hours with all the stops. Back at her apartment she could look for jobs—maybe a job in Pittsburgh. She pictured herself living harmoniously with Julian, like she'd done that one summer. Or maybe Jane would get big in the Art World and ask Fran to be her assistant. She imagined

Jane and Deena in bathing suits at Art Basel. Maybe one night they'd include her . . .

Fran found herself in line at a deli, heard herself ordering a sandwich. She saw her hand give the cashier a handful of bills. She felt herself chewing the sandwich. She floated above herself like one of Chagall's friendly women, lifted with sentiment and hope, except hers was more a detached feeling. She thought of Paulina from the magazine. Fran wouldn't allow herself to touch her hair, even to worry about her hair. Some people didn't even have hair! Some people were just heads! She wandered toward the ticket window. She would sleep and wake up in New York and everything would be different. She would let Paulina fix her hair. She would surrender. Anxiety fluttered in her stomach. She sneezed and strangers blessed her. She handed over her credit card and the Amtrak people restored her power.

16

On the train, Fran sat next to a guy her age who spent the trip talking across the aisle to his friend. The guy, who Fran gathered was named Brock, wore ripped jeans and had paint-spattered sneakers. His hair was in disarray, but his face was decent. Would he be the street punk who rescued Fran from predictable living? He paid her little attention.

Fran slept for hours, until she was woken by classical music booming from a cell phone. She looked at the Post-it for a long while. "He's like my guru," Brock told his friend, praising an eccentric, contradictory UCLA professor. Brock seemed familiar to Fran—not him exactly, but those like him. "Recipes ruin everything," he said. "Cooking is like painting . . ." Her ears twitched. Must be an art grad somewhere, she thought. Yale?

Everything he said made her dislike him more. "I've always wanted a pet monkey. You think we could keep it in studio?" His companion laughed at his every word. For a long stretch Brock was silent, underlining photocopies of theory with a grubby pencil, but then he started up again. "The first-years might go after us in crit. Remember how we were back then?"

The world he spoke of tempted Fran. She wished that Brock and his friend would accept her as one of their own, but they never even asked her name. She tried to summon the old painting fantasies—her grand debut at such-and-such gallery—but it no longer felt possible or important.

When their talking got too animated, she rose to change seats. The train jerked while Fran walked through the aisle. Her hand clumsily touched the shoulders of strangers. She passed women with children. People of all races. Who was she looking for? There were no open rows. She would have to choose someone to sit with. Pennsylvania passed by in blank fields and outdated little towns. Every few minutes her aimlessness would turn, like a coin catching light, and fill Fran with exhilaration. She would never go back to Ohio!

Her mind raced with possible outcomes. She braced herself for the worst—Paulina shunning her in front of her fancy friends. Paulina pushing her down an elevator shaft. Paulina surprised she's even there—the message was for someone else. No one at Paulina's because she's with Julian.

Fran walked the length of the train. Vast wastelands passed by the windows. The graffiti made her lonesome. Passengers unwrapped food from the dining car. Then, as happened every few years, like spotting an inexplicably big moon, Fran saw a beautiful boy.

He was dark haired. His features came from the same impossible place as Marvin's. He was with a friend. They seemed too young to see through her. Fran fell into the seat across from them and didn't wait for them to ask. "I'm Fran," she told them. The beautiful one rolled his eyes at her, like he was showing her how they worked. The beautiful never needed to speak, though sometimes they did Fran the favor.

"I'm Flip," the friend said, and pointed to the beauty. "This is Stephen." Stephen had it even worse than Marvin. He would never be able to blend in with a crowd.

They lived in Brooklyn. Flip told Fran all about the band they were in and gave her a business card. Every word they exchanged cemented their acquaintance. If Paulina didn't show, if the address was a fake, if the feeling was wrong, maybe she could bother these two. She hadn't told Gretchen she was coming. She hadn't told anyone. If Paulina killed her, no one would be able to say where she'd gone. Fran looked at the card in her hands. Braying Donkey, it said, and underneath it brayingdonkey.blogspot.com.

"What's that smell?" Stephen asked, finally revealing his voice.

"What smell?" asked Fran.

"It's like some chemical. Are you a scientist?" he asked her.

"She's a test question writer," Flip said, smiling at her.

"Actually, I'm a painter," Fran said, and Stephen lifted his beautiful face from Flip's shoulder. She smelled her hair; it smelled like iodine. "I think it's my hair. I just got it straightened."

"Why?" Stephen asked, rubbing his face. He looked into her eyes and she felt dissected.

"Long story," she said, hoping it made her seem mysterious, but Stephen just dozed against the window. For the rest of the ride she forged a bond with Flip. Flip was from San Francisco and had two brothers and two sisters. Fran could tell he was smarter than she was, but she didn't know if he was smart enough to know this. He was still so young.

When Stephen woke up, Flip said, "Guess what? Fran knows Apollo Space-Ears. She saw him naked!"

"Lots of times," Fran said.

"Cool," Stephen said, obviously impressed. "He filmed his new video in our friends' loft last year."

The train pulled into the dark labyrinth leading to Penn Station. The cabin went dark. Lights ran down Flip and Stephen's faces. Fran was terrified. They left the train together. *Like always*, Fran thought to herself, as if Flip and Stephen were her best friends and lovers and they all lived together in Brooklyn. She could go to all the Braying Donkey shows. She could even suggest a better name. They would record a whole album called *Fran*. A double album.

What was Paulina doing right now? Signing autographs? Slaughtering pigs? It was impossible to tell. Suddenly it crossed Fran's mind that Paulina could be throwing a party. Maybe the note was just an invitation and Paulina would be there with her *girlfriend*.

They took the long escalator up to the ground level. Everyone pulled rolling suitcases with one hand and held their cell phones in the other. Fran quickly sized them up as she had walking the train. She believed she could guess their life story from the style of their backpack—drama queen embarking on a singing career, college boy trying to find meaning in nature.

Inside Penn Station, some people kissed openly under the fluorescent lights; others ate muffins, displaced from the people they loved. It seemed impossible that any of the strangers could know Fran or would ever want to, though she continued to follow Stephen and Flip past the bathrooms and the pretzel stand, the small flower shop that distracted her back to the Lancaster fantasy.

Up the final set of escalators, Fran felt the evening air on her face like a lukewarm bath, and with it, a sense of accomplishment for having made it to the city. The city was important to so many people, though maybe, as she'd realized on the train, not to her. Fran stared at the majestic post office on Thirty-Fourth Street. A sweet smell from the mixed-nut cart was overpowered by the smell of urine as Fran followed Flip and Stephen past a pair of flattened jeans on the curb.

The sun had set and people leaving work late walked briskly past people on their way out to bars. Women walked jacketless into the cool night. Fran followed Flip and Stephen without looking at the street signs. She removed a long, straight hair stuck to her shirt. She pictured Paulina's girl-friend as Deena. "You wanna get a slice with us?" Flip asked. Fran nodded.

She held the Post-it in her pocket. Thinking about Paulina so impaired her nerves that she couldn't follow Flip and Stephen's conversation. All sound was skewed to her, like the fake world in a seashell.

"Who are you visiting again?" Stephen asked. Fran blushed.

"Her old friend," Flip said, "but she's not sure how it will go."

"I need the J train or the 6," Fran recited. Her stomach fluttered. She looked at Flip and Stephen distantly, as if they just happened to be eating pizza at her table.

"I should go now. She's expecting me." It was after nine

o'clock. Fran stood resolutely. Throwing her chewed pizza slice in a sidewalk trash can, she thought of a whole new set of worst scenarios—kissing Paulina and realizing she wasn't attracted to girls. Dating Paulina for months in a gay lie. Once, freshman year, Eileen had asked her if she was bi. "I don't know," she had answered. And she still didn't know.

When the subway car started moving, and the grimy tunnels spiraled away, Fran felt like she was in a robot's intestines. Another subway car appeared across from hers and Fran glimpsed the passengers through the speeding blurs of poles and metal and blackness. People she would never know, who she might have loved! Everyone was doomed. Fran listened to Stephen and Flip compare cell phone apps. She could still go to Paulina's later, she figured, but Paulina made her nervous.

Flip's room in his Greenpoint apartment reminded her of the college town. He'd taped quotes and paper scraps of encouragement on the drawers of his desk. On his walls were the old heroes—Lou Reed, Kurt Vonnegut—but also a signed Gorgeous Cyclops poster. "You really wanna hear us play?" Flip asked Fran again. Fran nodded enthusiastically. Stephen slunk across the room and got his guitar from its stand.

Singing woke Stephen from his daze, and Fran felt the full power of his charm. It was clear he was singing for someone not in the room (someone from his past?), or singing to his own unknowable future. They sang sweetly, and well; their voices fell into easy harmony with each other. Fran felt like she had discovered them, whatever that meant. She was starting to talk with them about music, which she knew little about, when their roommate Phil (short athletic build, glasses) appeared, insisting they all go out dancing together. "Jenny is meeting us there!" he yelled. The boys whooped.

"Where?" Fran asked. *The J train or the 6*, she thought again.

"Club Haywire," Flip said. "You'll love it."

"I wish I could," Fran said. "But I have that thing." Her voice trailed off like steps into a basement.

Fran stood on the dance floor in her black dress. Her shoes were good dancing shoes, ones that allowed her to slide but kept her from slipping. Stephen and Flip were in the back surrounded by girls. The song was an old soul song put to a new hip-hop beat. Everyone on the dance floor threw themselves into their dancing. Lights flashed over the crowd. Fran saw open spots where she could hold court without hitting anyone.

She swayed awkwardly. *Go on*, she told herself. There was a flamboyant boy dancing in the middle of the crowd, and she knew he would be fun to dance-battle with. But she felt a sinking in her knees. It's not the right people, Fran thought.

The song reached a bridge, a breakdown everyone danced

to, even the DJs behind their equipment. Stephen caught her eye and waved her onto the floor. He has no idea, Fran thought. He is totally oblivious to what I do on the dance floor. She imagined dancing with him, cutting up the air around him, play-fucking him without touching any part of him. But she couldn't move. Aches congregated in her ankles and hips. Her sinuses wove together in a stubborn knit. Stephen was persistent. He was wearing cool jeans. All the girls watched him. Fran tried to give him a provocative glare, but it came out a sad smile. She burned in her body. She could not dance.

Paulina sat in her living room with the television tuned to the live feed. The note had been a whim, almost a joke, but once she'd gotten back to the city she realized how badly she wanted Fran to show. All week long she'd wished she'd used a Sharpie. It was possible, even likely, that Julian had washed off the note unwittingly before Fran saw it. Still, something told her that Fran would make the trip. Paulina had filled her refrigerator with fancy things to eat. She'd made her bed herself and even cleaned the bathroom. Her maid had quit the week before, and Paulina hadn't yet replaced her. Harvey had a company he used, but they gave him different maids every week. Paulina liked consistency. She wanted someone accountable when her suede was ruined.

From ten o'clock to ten thirty, Paulina stared at the television expectantly. As the clock neared eleven, her mind played against her, and she started doubting Fran would show. She had so much nervous energy that when one of the cats ran by, Paulina chased after it. The cats had a whole life together; they rarely looked to Paulina for comfort. They watched her with cold lizard eyes. The white cat nuzzled the black one. Paulina was just their roommate, not their friend. She willed herself to stop glancing at the television. If Fran arrived, Paulina would hear the buzzer, or a knock, or Eugene would call up from the desk. Paulina sat purposefully in the dining room where she couldn't see the screen. It was a good screen, one of those plasma ones. It was alive, or something. She couldn't remember.

After trying on countless outfits, Paulina had settled on velvet leggings and a Proenza Schouler silk shirt that wrinkled with her every thought. Over the course of the last hour, the velvet had picked up lint and cat hair. Paulina resisted the urge to change, instead lowering herself to the carpet and attempting the exercises her personal trainer was always begging her to do. Jasmine said that Hank was a great lay, but with Paulina he was all business. He genuinely seemed to care about Paulina's health.

Paulina would offer Fran a glass of water. Or would they just immediately start kissing? Could they skip the talking? There was nothing to say, really. They could talk after. The first time would go pretty quick. Paulina pictured wild grasp-ing, probably with the lights on. Maybe they wouldn't even make it to the bedroom. Maybe on the living room couch. Paulina's phone buzzed with meaningless texts from Luca.

The exercises were exhausting. Crawling back to the living room couch, Paulina noticed a philosophy book Julian had given her with much ceremony. Its fat spine was visible under a pile of junk mail. I'll read when I'm dead, she thought.

Every time Paulina glanced at the television, there was some poor soul lingering by the desk. Old men, families, teen-agers, deliverymen. The camera faced Eugene, the doorman behind the desk, instead of the guests. It must have been a privacy measure. When the guests turned toward the elevator, Paulina saw their profiles.

Her weekend was totally free. Clive had invited her to brunch, but she'd refused to commit. It was always a scene at his place, one she'd grown bored of, though sometimes people there amused her—old eccentrics Clive had handpicked from his Botanica Ramses dealings. His style line was thriving, but she wasn't jealous. The fags will inherit the earth, she thought, and felt the corners of her lips twitch into a smile.

Paulina adjusted her breasts in her bra. There was food from Zabar's they could eat tomorrow, or she could easily get a table at L'Apicio by calling ten minutes before they left. The weather report showed possible rain for Saturday. They could just stay in. They'd have so much to catch up on. But afterward they'd pull themselves together and greet the world. Paulina could see them leaving her apartment, the pavement newly wet from rain, the leaves trembling in the breeze. They could go to an art museum, if Fran was still into art. Or Royce had a pretty wild collection in his apartment, if Fran wanted to lick a Warhol or something. Plus her own apartment had some good pieces. The Peter Halley painting in the bathroom had warped—whoops! Whatever. Luca said it couldn't be fixed. What, would they indict her for it? The skinny, old art people. Would they drag her to the gallows?

Paulina wondered if Fran still painted. She'd searched the Internet for both Frances and Francesca Hixon, finding mostly obituaries of ancient widows. Maybe she'd been painting her ass off. Maybe she'd want to stay for a while. Paulina would let her use the sunroom as a studio. It had great light and ventilation. But she was getting ahead of herself again. Fran was probably lying on Julian's chest in that stuffy Pittsburgh apartment. Fran lacked guts. Sometimes she was full of life and longing, but other times Paulina had found her as hollow as a decorative egg.

It was well past midnight, but Paulina didn't know the trains, how long it would take Fran to get there from whatever landfill she clung to in the Midwest. From what Julian said, it sounded like the poor thing worked in a factory all day. On-screen, two men struggled past the camera carrying a bureau. Eugene led them to the service elevator and pushed the button for them. Paulina knew Eugene well by now. She'd watched him pass his hand over his face when he was tired, and she knew the neck stretches he did every hour. He always spoke to the cleaning crew. He knew all the tenants. She'd seen the way he chatted with his replacements—a younger, trimmer man that worked mornings, and the large woman that worked the graveyard shift, who once kept Luca waiting until Paulina picked up her phone and vouched for him.

The second time would be more nuanced. They'd be high off each other by then. Paulina would show off all she could do. The third time, Fran would surprise her. Fran would learn quickly. She'd laugh in Paulina's arms. They'd eat between sessions and leave a huge mess in Paulina's kitchen. One that would never truly get cleaned up.

A woman caught her eye on the television. She was about Fran's size, but had long, straight hair. Paulina's phone vibrated with a text from the Curl Club. She turned back to the television and watched the woman wait near the elevators. Paulina couldn't make out her face. She stared at the woman's low-cut dress. Paulina was so prepared for a guest, so ready for adventure, that she considered going down to the lobby to meet the woman, or asking Eugene to send her up. Paulina imagined the woman lounging around her apartment. After hours of sex, an intimacy would form. Maybe they would even fall in love. But this was nonsense. If the last decade had taught her anything, it was that no other person would do. Besides, Fran was probably walking out of the subway this very minute. The woman hesitated by the elevators and seemed to change her mind, or maybe she had forgotten something. It was impossible to tell. Paulina watched the woman as she turned and walked past the doorman's table, through the revolving doors, to where Paulina could no longer see her.

Acknowledgments

Thank you to my Mom & Dad, and to all of my family, Buck's Rock, Flying Object, my editor Cal Morgan, my agent Claudia Ballard, Harper Perennial, Granta Books, Anne Meadows, *McSweeney's* and the Amanda Davis Highwire Fiction Award, Joanna Howard, Sandy Florian, Meredith Steinbach, Mairead Byrne, Karen Rile, Noy Holland & Sam Michel, Chris Bachelder, Peter Gizzi, Lynn Bailey, John Maradik, Adam Robinson, Blake Butler, Giancarlo Ditrapano, Barbara Galletly, Mojo Lorwin, Paradise Copies, Veronika, Erin, Brent, Asher, the Xperimental People, C. S. Ward, my FO classes, my Jersey friends, and the wonderful readers: Ahrum, Anita, Anna, Arda, Carla, Cat, Chain, Chelley, Chelotti, Deweese, Edward, Ehu, Eliza, EP, ES, Ezra, Guy, Halie, Heather, Ivan, Jacob, Jono, Julio, Landman, Lauren, Leidner, Luke, Madeline, Max, Mike, Nat, Noah, Phoebe, Sarah, Shannon, Susan, and Ted.